Bella's Rebellion

Short Stories

Ann Stanley

Copyright © 2016 by Ann Stanley

The short story, *Heritage*, previously appeared in *Mosaic: a Collection of Creative Writing by the Story Cartel*. *Bella's Rebellion* was published in *Fiction Break Favorites, Fall 2014, the Best of ShortFictionBreak.com*. Earlier versions of *Columns, Robotics, Lollypop* (as *Last One Standing*), *Flashback, Photo Shoot, The Affair*, and *Faded Jeans* were published on the online literary journal shortfictionbreak.com.

PUBLISHER'S NOTE

This is a work of fiction. Names, characters, places, and incidents either are the product of the author's imagination or are used fictitiously. Any resemblance to actual persons, living or dead, or to real events is entirely coincidental.

SPIDERMOON PUBLISHING

Paperback ISBN 978-1-945250-00-2

e-book ISBN 978-1-945250-01-9

annstanleywrites.com

Author photo by Carol Sternkopf Photography

For my amazing mother, who always encouraged me to have my own career, be my own person, and not let my gender stop me from anything I wanted to undertake.

Contents

INTRODUCTION

WELCOME TO MY first collection of short stories and flash fiction. All of them feature women and girls (in the case of *Astronomer's Child*, the 'woman' is a zephyr) learning from tough situations.

Some pieces deal with finding fulfillment, in particular by pursuing something which feeds the heart and soul. This topic comes out of my own struggles to find my passion. Some people seem to find their calling easily, to almost be born with the instinct that *this* is their path, whether it is dance (one of my nieces knew she would become a dancer when she was four), music (I know a young boy who lives for music), writing (again, I know those who sensed this from an early age), technology, science, business, or any of a million other possible careers. However, I am not one of those people, and I believe that most of us are not. Even if we are, we may be blocked from following that path by circumstances. This could be finances, parental biases, lack of access, or some tragedy. Perhaps we don't believe in ourselves, or in the possibility of making a living from art. Another theme I explore is kindness. This is especially strong in *Promoting Kindness*, in which I turn around the usual apoca-lyptic approach to a cataclysmic event, in this case global warming, and ask: what if one person started a movement to help others rather than attacking them? I feel strongly that humans have the potential to be either horrid to each other, or kind. Other stories examine the possibility of kindness through a variety of lenses, from a parent protecting a child, to an aunt helping a niece to see her mother in a different light, and a daughter helping her father deal with the death of his wife.

As I compiled these stories, I was surprised to see a thread of spying running through many of them. This is strongest in *Columns, Robotics,* and *The Affair*, but appears in subtle ways elsewhere in this volume. I am not sure why the idea appeals to me, but apparently it does.

I was also surprised to discover how much I deal with conflict between mothers and daughters. *Heritage* and *The Hoarder* both address a daughter's feelings about a dead mother, while in *Columns* the conflict is between a young woman and her mother.

Finally, there are a few odd-ball stories in which my sci-ence background emerges. I just couldn't keep these under wraps. I hope you'll enjoy the variety.

I've been asked why I chose *Bella's Rebellion* as the title story. First, I love the title. Second, this story captures so much of what I believe; that women need to assert them-selves, to be the heroines of their own stories, and to stretch and grow into their potential——be a little bit bold, even.

While one or two of these stories are based in my person-al experiences, none of the people, incidents, or settings are real. These are all works of fiction. In particular, my mother is nothing like any of the mothers who appear in my stories. Those mothers are completely imaginary.

February 2016   Ann Stanley

Bella's Rebellion

ROBOTICS

NANCY STARED AT the statistics from her project. *What am I doing wrong? It should work; I'm sure of it.* But the data was clear: her new algorithm did not correctly identify any more people than her old one did.

A knock on the door of her office interrupted her thoughts, and she swiveled in her chair to find Dr. Julius Friedlander smiling at her.

She blushed. She had a thing for tall, skinny nerds, and Dr. Friedlander, a year younger than herself despite his fame, was her type. Definitely her type. She'd had a slight crush on him ever since she'd started her postdoc at Williams Research.

He bobbed his head slightly and stepped into the room. "Do you have time to talk?"

She gulped and said, as calmly as she could, "Sure."

"Great." He smiled widely and sat on the corner of her desk, his long legs crossed, one foot dangling.

Too shy to say anything, she studied his hands. He had the strong, slender fingers of a pianist.

"This won't take long. I know you're busy." He cleared his throat and she glanced up to meet his beautiful blue eyes and thick dark lashes.

A little fire started in her chest. She fought with herself. *This is not the time and place. He's a co-worker. Stop it.* She pretended to stare at her computer screen. "Please, go ahead."

He picked up a pen and studied it. "I learned that your software can identify people by their body language, even when they undergo surgery to disguise their faces and voices." The dark hair falling over his thin face sent a thrill through her.

"Sometimes."

"Not just sometimes. It picked Abrahim Mosher out of a line at airport security. If it hadn't, who knows what would have happened; security never would have stopped him, with the explosives hidden inside his artificial knee."

"Hip."

"Right. Look," he tapped the pen on the desk, "I'm working on a project which might need your expertise. I'd like to know more about your concept, and why it succeeds even when facial recognition software fails. How can you pick a man like that out of a crowd?"

"Before I went to graduate school, I worked for a private detective. He recognized people from the back and side, even when he couldn't see their faces. He said it was the way they moved and held themselves. He was rarely wrong, even if they'd had an accident, or had been sick."

"Hmm. Actors know that, of course. They take on the movements and gestures of their characters."

"And animators study hours of film to get body language correct and character-specific."

"So what prevents a man from changing the way he moves?"

"It can be done, but it's a lot of effort. Few can keep it up all of the time, or cover all aspects of their behavior. For example, you like to hold something and tap it."

He set the pen on the desk quickly and she laughed. "You can stop for the moment, but you're also swinging your leg. Put those gestures together, along with—"

"Voice, height—"

"Right. And, remember, it doesn't have to be perfect, just

enough to send in the police or airport security to check."

"Brilliant, Dr. Olsen. Brilliant. I'll set up a meeting next week to tell you about our project, and see if you're interested." He stood and reached out to shake her hand.

When she took it, he held on for a second too long, and she felt energy move between them. *Well, he isn't married.*

Just as he reached the door, he turned very casually, and invited her to a party at his house, as if it were an afterthought. "Bring a friend."

FRIDAY NIGHT, NANCY and her best friend, Kristi, dressed for the party: Nancy in a dark blue shift which floated easily over her thin, athletic body, and Kristi in a gray, low-cut sweater and hip-hugging black pants to show off her curves. They giggled, gossiping about the men at work as they drove across the mountains to the coast. Julius's house was a small wooden cottage on the beach, with an open downstairs, a loft bedroom reached by a spiral staircase, and a wrap-around wooden porch.
As soon as they entered and saw the staircase, they ran up it.

"This place must have cost a fortune," Kristi whispered as they pressed their noses against one of the many upstairs windows, admiring the sunset.

"It isn't very big."

"Yeah, but these views don't come cheap."

"Hello, ladies," Julius interrupted them, placing a hand on Nancy's shoulder. "Thanks for coming."

She looked up to see him hunched over a martini in his other hand, his gaze out the window. Did the man ever stand up straight? She supposed that when you were six-foot-something, it was harder to stand straight, but her years of doing her best to hold herself erect in ballet classes made her want to put her hand on his back and push him tall. That, and the intense desire to touch him. But she resisted. "Thanks for the invitation. This place is like a fairy tale."

His face darkened as he stared straight ahead. "My parents built it before I was born. They were killed in a car accident last year."

"I'm so sorry."

He shrugged and looked down at her. "I miss them terribly. But I do love it here."

Nancy introduced her friend. "She works in the biology lab at Williams."

Kristi smiled up at him coquettishly, and, just for a second, Nancy regretted bringing her along. She was so sexy, with her blond hair, her full breasts, and her rosebud lips.

Certainly, when they went out together on the weekends, the men clustered around her and ignored Nancy. What had she been thinking? Julius would probably fall for Kristi, and she'd hate her forever for stealing the man she wanted. She'd lose both her best friend and her chance for love.

Luckily, Kristi didn't seem interested in Julius. She turned back to the ocean, and said, "I'm just a tech."

"Well, nice to meet you. I'd better go check on the others." And Julius left, apparently not stunned by Kristi's beauty.

"You should see your face," Kristi said, and giggled. "Don't worry, I'm not interested. He's a geek, all elbows and stiff bearing. I prefer men who are comfortable in their bodies."

However, later that evening, while Nancy was standing downstairs watching people filing about, she saw Kristi and Julius climbing the silver staircase together, and she wondered. She decided to follow them, but her hand had barely touched the cable which served as the handrail when she was interrupted by a large older man in a cream-colored suit. "You must be Dr. Olsen," he said. "I'm Karl Hansen from MIT, and I hear you've done some amazing work."

Karl Hansen, the famous developer of the health shirt

which tracked at least twenty important biological measurements, held out his hand and she shook it.

He led her to a couch next to an ocean-facing glass window. Star-struck, she chatted about research and nearly forgot all about Julius and Kristi until it was time to go. Then she found her friend outside on the deck with one of the better-looking research assistants, a guy named Mark who spent all of his spare time on a surfboard.

On the way home, Kristi said, rather seriously, "I've agreed to be a research subject for Julius's project. Did he tell you about it? It's very exciting."

"Is that what you two were discussing upstairs?"

"Uh-huh. Oh, you, don't be jealous. It's nothing. I just mentioned my desire to do something for my country, something more than analyzing that DNA from Europe, and he got all excited and asked me to help. He said his experiment is top-secret, and he needs some volunteers with security clearances."

"For what?"

"Something to do with miniature robots. He said he'd tell you all about it later in the week."

Her words worried Nancy. Dr. Hansen had told her they were starting to put micro scale robots into people's brains, to take out problem areas or insert chemicals. Later, she would wish more than anything that she'd warned her friend the technology was still unreliable, but she'd only nodded, pleased that her friend was more interested in Mark than Julius.

ON MONDAY, SHE cornered Kristi and took her to lunch in downtown Gilroy, the closest city to their lab. It didn't have much to offer in the way of food, but they had a favorite soup and sandwich place. They sat outside at a corner table with their salads, enjoying the late spring weather.

"I went out with Mark Saturday night," Kristi said. "He's kind of a dork."

"That's not why I paid for your lunch, and you know it."

"What? Don't you wanna hear all about the waves all up and down the coast right now?"

"Nah. What happened this morning in the lab?"

"I broke a ten-thousand-dollar beaker?" Her friend tried to hold her grin, but Nancy knew she was teasing.

"Come on."

Kristi put her finger over her mouth and wiggled her eyes back and forth, as if hunting for spies. "Shhh, top secret."

They were sitting ten feet from the only other diners

outside. "Oh, God. No one can hear us."

"Julius is full of of hot air. I don't know what you see in him."

"Okay, so you're not going to tell me. You owe me lunch, big time."

"Come on, don't be a hard ass."

Nancy waved her fingers at her, as if asking for money. "Let's see, your salad was twenty-five, and that latte you're drinking—"

Kristi shook her head as if disgusted with her friend, then smirked. "All right, all right. He made me read a stack of papers about consent and sign them. There was another employee there, a guy named Luke. I believe he dates your receptionist."

"Yeah. They were at the party, too."

"So Luke and I watched a little video, and signed a stack of papers, then Ulrick—do you know him?"

"Not really. Big blond guy, right?"

"Yeah. Quiet. Anyway, he put some drops in our eyes. That's all."

"What was in those drops? Robots?"

"How'd you guess?"

"Shit. Those robots could be dangerous. Why'd you

agree?"

"I told you. I needed to do something to help stop ISIS from destroying us."

Nancy sipped her iced tea and studied her. "What's that got to do with Julius?"

"Can't tell you. Really. Please don't make me break my word. They'll let you know everything on Wednesday."

"Fine. But you owe me a drink."

"A great band's playing up in San José Friday night. Wear your mini skirt and go-go boots."

Nancy laughed at their easy shift from ISIS to dancing. They understood each other so well that they didn't have to dwell on details. Wasn't that what great friendships were about?

SHE'D NEVER BEEN in the top secret conference room before. Like all of their conference rooms, it had an oval table with chairs around it in the center, but there was far more equipment scattered around the edges than in the unclassified rooms. She took a seat and waited as Julius logged into the secure network and a screen descended from the ceiling. A diagram appeared on the screen.

"This," Julius said, "is the basic idea. We need to put spies into areas controlled by ISIS, but it's way too dangerous to send in a person, after all of the recent executions. Drones are out because they are too obvious, and they tend to eventually fail; we cannot risk having the enemy get his hands on one. So our task was to find another way."

The door clicked open and Ulrick entered, carefully closing it behind him. He took a seat next to Nancy and nodded. She had met this broad-shouldered man only once before, at last year's Christmas party, so all she knew was that he was a neuroscientist of sorts, and he'd put drops containing robots in her friend's eyes.

Julius turned back to the screen. "I thought we should plant bugs on members of ISIS, but it had to be something they couldn't find and remove. A robot would be nice, if it could somehow crawl onto them, because obviously it's too dangerous to send in a person."

Ulrick stood and walked over to the computer. "That's where I come in. I've been working with the robotics group at MIT to design nano-scale robots which can enter the brain and find cancer cells or other pathologies. It occurred to me that we could do something similar with the optic and auditory nerves. We know enough now to interpret signals from these nerves and turn them back into pictures and sounds."

Something clicked in Nancy's brain, and she shivered at the thought. "Oh, so that's the real reason Dr. Hansen has spent so much time here?"

Julius didn't blink or nod.

An itch crept from her neck to her fingertips and she stiffened.

Ulrick spoke, his voice harsh in the nearly-empty room. "Maybe she doesn't have the spine for this."

Julius stared blankly at her. "Is that true? Do you want to leave now, before we tell you anything important?"

"No." She shook her head. These men fascinated her, even as they creeped her out.

A new photo flashed up on the screen. It was a robot next to a ruler. Nancy gasped; it was less than a micron in diameter. It was replaced on the screen by a mouse, its bright eyes, black nose, and long grey whiskers looking straight at her.

Ulrick walked over and pointed at it. "Figuring out how to target the appropriate nerves was easy. Getting it into a living being was harder. We couldn't plan on doing brain surgery. Instead, the robot had to somehow crawl in on its own. So I went back to MIT, where the robotics experts have been working on this very issue. Brain surgery is dangerous and expensive, so they have developed robots which can enter through the eyes and nose."

"Dr. Hansen told me about that." Nancy's thoughts were flying a mile a minute by now.

"He's been involved with the mouse experiments," Julius said. "What you'll see next are some of his results. This is a video from the devices which implanted themselves in this mouse."

Silver bars came into view, then jittery movement, a piece of food picked up in mouse paws, and, with it all, the sound of scraping and unintelligible voices. The video ended.

"You're going to use mice to invade ISIS?" Nancy asked, surprising even herself with the question.

Julius laughed. "No, of course not." He flashed up a flow chart and replaced Ulrick next to the screen. "We haven't figured this part out, but we'll somehow drop small carrier robots, filled with these tiny guys, near where we suspect our enemies are. The robots will have enough power to crawl up to five miles, seeking human DNA."

"In theory," Ulrick said. "That part isn't worked out yet."

Julius smiled. "True. But we think we can solve that issue."

"What's your part in this?" Nancy asked.

"He programs the robots," Ulrick said. "There are, what, Julius? About a hundred people in on this project?"

"I think so. Everything from biologists to the strategists at the Pentagon." Julius frowned at her. "It's a hard problem, creating robots too small to be seen, able to crawl over obstacles, and yet having enough power to go that far while targeting humans."

"Wow!"

He cracked a tiny smile. Once again, she felt the power of his eyes on her and swallowed hard. Then he turned back to the screen. "It's all a bit far-fetched, but it's also a big deal. So, anyway, when they get to a person, the carrier opens a compartment, a handful of smaller bots come out, crawl up the body, and release the micro invaders."

"Are you guys nuts? This'll never happen. Even if it does, why do you need me?" Nancy stared at the diagram, incredulous.

Ulrick laughed. "Yes, it will. These bots will be fantastically cheap to produce. The technical problems are all solvable. Believe me."

Julius gave her a wider smile. Seeing it, she settled back in her chair, letting the energy flow between them. Even if she chose not to join this project, just being here a while longer could lead to something good.

He winked and her heart almost stopped. Then he walked back to the computer. "What we're going to show you next is absolutely top secret. Also, I suspect you won't be happy with some of it. Please understand that you cannot share this with anyone."

He was looking at the screen, the frown back between his brows. Nancy shivered. Despite her attraction to him, she half wished she could leave.

"Our next step was to test the technology in humans," Ulrick said. "As you saw, it worked well in mice. We were delighted that they didn't suffer any ill-effects."

"None at all? How do you know?" Nancy was intrigued. She didn't know much about biology, but it seemed amazing that the bots could attach themselves to the nerves and relay their signals without any issues.

"Well," Ulrick swallowed. "I hope you aren't squeamish."

"I'm not."

"We tested over two hundred mice. We sacrificed two every day. On average, the robots disintegrated and washed out of their systems at one month, with all of them gone by two months. The mice we didn't kill lived out their normal lifespan."

"So you thought it would be safe to try people." Nancy shifted uncomfortably in her seat.

"Yes. We got the go-ahead to infect six, to test safety, not that safety is our primary concern. If a few terrorists die, oh well."

"But you didn't test it on terrorists, did you?" She folded her arms around herself, worrying about Kristi, the robot carrier.

Julius gave her a dark look. She didn't care. She wanted to absorb the import of what they'd done.

Julius paced. "Look, you can't blame Ulrick and me. We didn't design this test, although I was involved in persuading our first test subjects."

Ulrick took a chair across from her and studied her face. "Because of the top-secret nature of the project, we couldn't advertise for volunteers. This isn't a cure for lung cancer. We thought for a long time about how to recruit them."

Julius brought up another diagram. "After much discussion, the NSA ordered us to find two people of a patriotic bent, with security clearances, and ask them. We couldn't have anyone running around telling the world they had robots in their heads. We held a party, and asked our friends to bring their friends."

Nancy leaned forward in her chair, sitting up as tall as she could, furious. "You used me."

"I suppose you could say that." He shrugged. "But Kristi was delighted to help her country in the war against terrorism. If you want, I can play the clip of her agreeing to the robots. I vetted her very carefully to ensure she was a good choice."

"I'll watch it later."

"The robots are perfectly safe," Ulrick said.

"Yeah, right. You put gadgets in her brain, and you expect me to believe they can't cause problems?" She pushed her chair away from the table and glared at the two men.

Julius' face softened. "I won't lie to you. Sure, there's a small risk."

"Why didn't you use soldiers? Why our friends?" Nancy had never been hysterical, but she felt like she might give it a try.

"The military wouldn't let us," Ulrick said. "You know, Julius, this was a bad idea. I told you so."

She looked wildly back and forth between them. Julius nodded, and Ulrick took a hypodermic needle out of his pocket, along with a vial.

Her eyes grew big. "What's that?"

"It'll wipe out your short term memory. This conversation will be history."

"Is that why my friend couldn't tell me much about the robots? You gave her that drug?"

Ulrick shook his head. "No. We didn't. We just made her understand how important it is that no one outside the project knows about them. If you aren't on board—"

Much as she hated the thought of Kristi carrying around these robots, Nancy wanted to know more. "No, no, guys, don't do this. I'm okay. Really."

Ulrick set the needle on the table and looked at her face. She saw him tracing its outlines, studying her as if to determine whether or not she could be trusted. She glanced up and realized that Julius was doing the same thing.

After what seemed like forever, Ulrick nodded. "If you show any more signs of cracking, we'll make sure you don't remember a thing. Continue, Julius."

A video began. Although the visuals were fuzzy and jerky, she thought she recognized a painting on Kristi's office wall. The view changed to a computer screen and then to some hands. That was definitely the ring her best friend always wore.

"Oh, my God. I'm looking through Kristi's eyes!"

"Yes."

She heard what sounded like Kristi's voice, then someone else, but she couldn't quite make out their words. Whenever Kristi turned her head, the world blurred.

Julius paused the video. "This is where we need you. Can you clean it up and run it through pattern recognition software?"

She hesitated, considering what the success of this project could mean for her country, and how little she could do to prevent harm from coming to Kristi, then nodded. "Sure. Although it'll be harder when there's more background noise and people are walking around."

"I believe in you. We'll need to match what we find to the data collected on terrorists, too."

"Can do."

"Does this mean you're in?" Julius asked, his eyes searching her face. "You can't go all soft on us in the very unlikely event that something happens to your friend."

Kristi would be fine, if the mouse research held for people. Why wouldn't it? The robots would disintegrate in less than a month. In the meantime, maybe she'd get to know this intriguing man a little better. "Yes, I'm in."

OVER THE NEXT few days, she received an in-depth tour of the project and the information they'd been collecting. Then she set to work. It was a little weird hanging out with Kristi after seeing through her eyes and hearing through her ears, but she never listened in for long. Her job was to create software to interpret the sounds the robots sent her way, not to spy on her friend's life. Still, it was emotionally easier to use the recordings from Luke. Besides, he worked in a noisy environment, so the software had to be extremely precise to pick out words and images from the background.

AT NINE PM the following Friday, three weeks after the robots had been implanted in Kristi's eyes and ears, Nancy arrived at Kristi's apartment, ready to go dancing at their favorite club. She'd worn her hottest outfit, a low-cut red top with skinny jeans that fit her perfectly, wanting Julius to drool if he happened to be watching through Kristi's eyes, as he sometimes did.

She was surprised to see that Kristi had on a long-sleeved T-shirt and shapeless khakis.

"Let's go," Kristi said.

What was wrong with her? "You can't go dancing in that!"

"Why not?"

"It's awful. Wear your black miniskirt with those stripped leggings."

"But I need to be comfortable. I have a headache. "

"How come?" Was the headache from the devices in Kristi's brain? She didn't dare say anything; she didn't want to frighten her friend unnecessarily.

"Just work. It was hectic today."

Nancy hoped that was it. She swayed her hips, as if dancing. "You'll feel better after we get out there. Hurry up and change. Let's go."

Kristi went into the bathroom to take a couple of aspirin. A minute later, Nancy heard a moan, then a thump. She raced to the door. Her friend lay on the floor, her eyes open, rolled up into her head.

By the time the ambulance arrived, Kristi was dead. The doctors said an aneurism had burst in her brain, but Nancy wondered.

She called work and told the receptionist about Kristi's death. "I'll be out indefinitely." She hardly got the words out before she broke down, sobbing.

Kristi's parents had already arrived from Wisconsin, but they were in no shape to make any decisions. Kristi made funeral arrangements, called relatives and friends for them, and helped organize Kristi's affairs. She'd never realized there was so much to take care of when someone died. Friday afternoon, while she was emptying the closet in Kristi's bedroom, Julius walked into the room and cleared his throat.

"I am so sorry about your friend," he said.

She shrugged. If she replied to him, she'd burst into tears. Instead, she pointed towards what used to be Kristi's office, where her friend did art projects. "Her mother is in there. Tell her."

"I will. But first I want to talk to you, somewhere private."

"My place? I'm close by."

"Too risky. Walls have ears."

"I can't go to work right now."

"Fine. Let's go for a drive."

He took her across the mountains to his beach house. When she climbed the silver staircase and stared at the view, she didn't see it; she was crying too hard.

He wrapped his arms around her. "I know what you're thinking, but I don't believe it's possible. The robots are too small. In any case, she must have already had the aneurism. You do know that, don't you?"

She turned to him then, and he kissed her gently, then more passionately. Before she knew it, they were naked together on his bed.

"You're so beautiful and so brilliant," he said. "I've wanted you ever since I met you."

She spent every night with him after that, mostly crying while he hugged her. Their love-making helped, but it could never truly ease the loss of her closest friend.

GOING BACK TO work after two weeks away, she was uneasy about the robotics project, but she tried to tell herself that Kristi's aneurism had nothing to do with with the little robots in her brain. Then, two days later, Luke had a small hemorrhagic stroke. He would recover, but it was too much of a coincidence for Nancy.

She stormed down the hall to Julius's office. His door was closed. She knocked. There was no answer, so she grabbed the doorknob and twisted. To her surprise, because he always locked it when he wasn't there, the door popped open. Julius was slumped over his desk. She shouted, "Julius, are you okay?" He didn't move. She tapped his back, but there was still no reaction.

Just as she reached for his throat to feel his pulse, Ulrick burst through the door.

"Oh, God," he said. "I worried Julius would go next. He insisted on putting the robots in his own eyes and ears. I tried to stop him, but he said he couldn't do it to someone else if he wasn't willing to do it to himself."

"How did you get here so fast?"

"I heard his head drop onto the desk, and then I heard your voice coming out of my computer. He must still be alive. The robots tap into the cellular matrix for their energy."

"Call 911. I'll see if he has a pulse." Panicked, it took her a minute to find the right spot. When her cold hand touched it, he groaned.

"He's alive," she said, half crying, half so angry about this stupid project she wanted to slap either Julius or Ulrick.

Later, as she waited nervously in the emergency room, she wondered if there was any way to send Ulrick to jail for Kristi's murder. Probably not, since the top-secret nature of the project meant no one besides a select few would ever know why she had died.

After a long wait, the nurse called her over. "He's hemorrhaging somewhere around his auditory nerve. We're wheeling him into surgery now. You might as well leave."

Nancy phoned Ulrick from her car. He must have heard the panic in her voice, because he said, "He's a strong guy. He'll be okay. And, just so you know, we're closing down this project. Go home. Take care of yourself."

By evening, they learned that Julius would probably survive, but he might never fully recover.

THAT WAS IT. She was done, not just with this project, but also with Williams Research Center, and even the entire country. She sent her resumé to a company in France which used pattern recognition for environmental purposes. They flew her over for an interview and offered her a job on the spot. Her French wasn't good, but she could learn.

The last time she climbed the silver staircase, Julius was lying on his side, staring at the ocean, while his full-time nurse busied herself on the far side of the room, pretending to give them some privacy. He was better, though he continued to have trouble with short-term memory and motor control. Nancy sat on the edge of his bed and picked up his hand. "I'm leaving tomorrow, sweetheart."

He didn't respond, but tears rolled down his cheek, so she knew he'd heard her. That was an improvement; he'd been deaf for the past month. She kissed his cheek and stood, but he grasped her hand hard and spoke, his voice hoarse. "I'm so sorry about Kristi and about us. I wanted us to work out."

Her breath quickened. She tightened her hand on his, and then pulled away. "You know where to find me." Then she left, quickly descending the spiral staircase.

LOLLYPOP

"Ha, ha, I win," I shouted. Everyone else sat up. I was still standing, the last one left in the game we'd been playing.

My mother walked over and gave me my prize: a huge multicolored lollypop.

"Aww," Charles said. "I wanted that."

"I'll share," I said. Each of my friends and siblings popped up from where they lay, shook the grass off their clothes, and ran over to us. They looked hungrily at the treat, and I considered how to break the hard candy. It came to me: I'd use Dad's hammer to smash it.

I set the sucker on the picnic table. "Be right back," I shouted over my shoulder and ran around the house towards the tool shed.

Dad and the other fathers huddled around the shed,

sitting on lawn chairs, with beer cans in their hands. They stopped talking when I approached.

The sight of those men took my voice away. I knew that Charlie's dad used his belt to punish Charlie, because Charlie had shown me the welts on his bottom one day. Susannah's father was worse. He was huge, with a loud voice and a funny way of looking at me. All the girls whispered about him when Susannah wasn't around. Some claimed he liked to get little kids alone and do bad things to them.

I didn't need the hammer enough to face them. I turned to run back to the party, but a big paw grabbed my shoulder.

"What's up, birthday girl?" Susannah's father's voice boomed in my ear. "Can we help you?"

The men laughed in a way I didn't like, a way that spoke of mysterious things I knew nothing about. I shrunk down inside myself, trying to be as small as possible.

But then my dad stood. "Leave her alone, Matt," he said. He put his arm around my waist and kissed my cheek. "How's it feel to be seven?" he asked.

It'd felt great when I'd won the game, but now I wished that I could stay six, safe from mean men, with their dangerous behavior and their horrid jokes. I leaned into him, but even Dad didn't feel strong enough to protect me anymore.

He walked me around to the front yard where the other kids were playing tag, as if he knew, somehow, all that had transpired in those few seconds and wanted to turn me back into his naïve, pampered little girl.

I saw the candy, and remembered the hammer. It seemed like a thousand years had passed, but the other kids didn't know that I'd done more than turn seven that day. I wanted them to still believe in the kid who'd left them only five minutes before. "Can you break the lollypop so everyone can have a piece?" I asked my father.

"Of course, pumpkin."

With those words, color returned to the world. I ran to join my friends, but I never forgot those moments in the backyard.

ASTRONOMER'S CHILD

IT HAD NO mother or father, unless you could count the young researcher driving up to the observatory on that clear summer afternoon in his old pickup.

The truck sent rocks flying off the dirt road. Perhaps one of those small pieces of granite could be more truthfully considered the father, for it struck a larger rock, birthing a spark. The fierce midwife from the desert blew the spark into life against a desiccated patch of grass.

The researcher, like so many fathers throughout the ages, never noticed the baby he'd help germinate. He drove on-ward to the small telescope, his only concern the rattlesnakes sunning themselves, their bodies thick on the warm open space of the road. He hated hearing the crunching of their spines beneath his wheels, yet there was little point in trying to avoid them. If all went well, he'd have the data he needed for his Ph.D. thesis, and he wouldn't need to return, at least not until after winter had sent the snakes into hibernation.

The tiny flame, only a few minutes old, grew quickly. Soon it was large enough to create its own children. First was a sage bush, the oil in its bark crackling and sputtering. A dead flower caught next, the flame quickly dying, leaving only a little black smudge on the ground to mark its short life. Perhaps these would have been the fire's only offspring, if the midwife hadn't sprung into action, using a strong gust to send sparks westward. Like sperm unable to reach an egg, none of them fertilized anything. The wind gave it one more go. This time a dead oak caught and exploded.

The mountain erupted in flames. Hungry tongues of red and orange tried to eat the sky. The growing fire shook its limbs in defiance and reared high into treetops left dehydrated by a rainless summer.

Ignoring the rattlers, deer fled along the road toward the observatory, then down the slopes to the north and towards the trickle of water at the base of the cool canyon. Raccoons and coyotes left the shade of their dens to follow them, while snakes and mice burrowed into dens.

South of the mountain, people stopped their cars and

stared upward, horrified, yet slightly enchanted by the colorful fingers of the fire-child. An old man watering his lawn
ran inside and called emergency.

The fire grew. Sirens blared as the forest service sprang to
life. Helicopters puttered off to assess the extent of the con-
flagration. Radios sputtered with news, and experts assessed
the danger, then called in a firefighting team, who hurried to
dig ditches and create firebreaks.

Another helicopter was dispatched to evacuate observatory staff. When their transportation arrived, the unwitting
progenitor and all of the staff protested. They didn't want to
leave their vehicles, or this important facility, to burn. However, their impatient rescuers overrode their objections with
warnings that the blaze could arrive soon. Even if it didn't,
smoke inhalation could kill them.

While this drama built, the newborn fire didn't even
notice. With the aid of its midwife-turned-nursemaid, it
roared westward, shaking its fists, excreting black smoke.
Reaching a patch of trees, it grew bigger, crisping them into
black spikes.

As night fell, the nursemaid calmed and angled south,
sending a protective shield of smoke into the valley. After
this, it would be difficult to see more than the glow of her

charge from the city below, perhaps saving it from the fire-
fighters who struggled to choke off its life.

Mountainside, the residents awoke, coughing. With burning eyes, they rose to prepare for work and school, even
though it seemed like night outside, the light of the sun
blocked by the thick smoke. As they gathered in their offices
and classrooms, they groused. Yesterday, they'd had a pretty
fire to watch, today they had only a red coal on the horizon
to entertain them while they coughed and wheezed, herding
their sensitive children into artificially-filtered air. Emergency
rooms filled with the asthmatic and old.

At three in the afternoon, the sun, which had finally
emerged overhead that morning, turned purple and green as
it slowly sank beneath the smoke. Birds roosted, as if night
had already arrived.

With the nanny blowing furiously west again, the child
grew into a magnificent adult. More and more acres fell to its
insatiable appetite.

Desperate, its enemies called in hotshot teams from far
away to join the fight. Animals fled east, up and down nearly
impassible slopes, some breaking legs in their panic. Those
who could not escape roasted alive, as the fire licked its
chops.

If the winds held, residents learned, their homes would stay safe, but the observatory might fall. Certainly, the newscasters announced, it would be a week before this mountain dragon could be tamed. Those people who could arranged to leave. They piled into cars and vans, carrying suitcases, heading to the homes of friends and relatives, or even hotels, far away.

The young fire eyed the vacant houses, longing to gobble up their wooden walls. Every night, the winds herded it that way for a little while, but every morning the air currents forced it westward until it met a blackened area it couldn't leap. Despite blowing harder and harder, the zephyr could not send a single spark far enough to bridge the gap and save her ward from nearly starving to death just short of a lovely glade of oaks only two hundred yards away.

Water dumped from helicopters onto the adolescent's edges. To survive, it buried itself deep in the ground in the roots of the trees and the underside of logs. If the winter ahead was mild, if the rains and snows never came, it might be able to revive itself next summer, or the summer after that, and cross that divide to consume trees and bushes and that delicious-looking building in the distance, with its shiny white dome.

In a year or two, perhaps three, native brush and flowers would reappear. Snakes and mice would crawl out of their holes. Deer and raccoon would return to eat the new growth, coyotes to eat the mice. Trees that needed fire to re-seed would sprout. And, one day, a spark would birth another child for the wind to raise.

HERITAGE

Sunday morning after Mass, Josephine laid the lawyer's letter on the coffee table in her little living room, then went into her kitchen and made a tray with tea and a *pain au chocolat* from her favorite bakery. She let her hair out of the tight bun she always wore in public, ran her fingers through it, and carried the tray to the table.

The letter had arrived on Tuesday, but she'd left it lying unopened on the front hall table, sure it had something to do with her mother, who had died in the fall. She'd bitten her lip every time she passed it, then stiffened her already tight shoulders and resolved not to let it bother her. Still, she'd found herself snapping at her physics students on Thursday. "Do you call this homework?" She'd flung the papers she'd graded the night before on her desk. "Were any of you listening in class when we covered the material? I doubt it. You could have read the chapter, but no, you did not. I want you to redo it tonight. Be prepared for a quiz tomorrow."

"Awww, Ms. Fondant, please," one of the girls had said. "A bunch of us are in the orchestra. We have a concert tonight."

Normally, Josephine would have postponed the quiz until Monday, given that music students were often her best pupils, but not this time. "This is a college prep class. Do all of you understand what that means? Don't expect me to coddle you." Josephine had pulled her cardigan tightly around her broad shoulders, sat up straight, and glared at the teenagers, her head throbbing.

They'd filed out of the room in silence, their shoulders rounded miserably. After they'd left, she'd regretted being so curt with them; it wasn't like her to lose control. It was that damn letter.

TAKING A SIP of her tea and a bite out of her pastry, she stared at the lawyer's letter. Her stomach hurt, as if she'd been punched in the gut. Finally, the *pain au chocolat* finished, she wiped her hands on her napkin, opened the envelope and read. To her surprise, her mother had left her a house in

Pittsburgh, less than one hundred and fifty miles away.

How could she have lived so close and never even called? Did she even know where I lived? Because I never knew where she was, the bitch.

It would be so easy to drive over some weekend and burn it down. The possibility was tempting. But Josephine was used to disciplining herself. She would arrange for someone to clean out the place and sell everything for her.

She spent all of February interviewing a variety of people for the job. None of them seemed right. One man struck her as too unreliable, while another seemed too picky. All wanted a bigger percentage than she wanted to give. Finally, she settled on a pair of women who seemed more experienced and organized than the others. She phoned to arrange their services.

"Hello, this is Linda with Your Right Hand Woman."

"This is Josephine Fondant. We spoke recently about my mother's house."

"Oh, yes. The one in Pittsburgh. Have you decided to hire us?"

"Yes. I'd like you to start right away."

"Oh, dear, I'm afraid that's impossible. We're very busy until September, but we could put you on the schedule then."

Josephine ground her teeth. "You said you were available

in April."

"I'm sorry if we misled you."

"Never mind," Josephine said and hung up, an uncomfortable sensation creeping up her spine. She couldn't stand people who let her down. People like her mother.

To calm herself, she reorganized her kitchen. By the time every cupboard was spotless, she accepted that, if she wanted the job done right, she would have to do it herself. She dropped by the garden shop where she worked summers and told them she'd be in Pittsburgh this year.

In any case, as the flowers bloomed and the days grew longer, her mind filled with a thousand questions about the mother she hadn't seen since she was sixteen. Surely the house would reveal the woman.

THE LAWYER HAD sent photos, so she easily picked out the two-story house from the others in the neighborhood. She probably would have known it anyway, since weeds filled its yard. Gritting her teeth, she exited her car and walked up to the front door. When she opened it, she stopped short in surprise. An oil painting of flamenco dancers hung in the foyer over an antique table with a lovely vase on it. Exploring, she discovered antique furniture, oriental carpets, and artwork in every room except the kitchen and a large nearly empty room at the back of the house. That room looked like some kind of dance salon, with no windows, a beautiful wood floor, and a wall of little shelves packed with CDs and a stereo. There was an attic, too, with one of those pull-down staircases, but, since it didn't open easily, she left that for later; she was already overwhelmed.

She sank onto the leather couch in the living room and dropped her head into her hands. Her mother must have been rich to buy all of these expensive things. She also must have spent a lot of time here. Why, in the twenty-three years she'd apparently owned this place, hadn't she ever picked up the phone and called her?

Josephine pushed her feelings back into the place she'd hidden them most of her life and stood. Time to do what she knew best: organize.

FOR WEEKS, SHE emptied closets, chests, and cabinets. She sold large quantities of expensive clothes, textiles, and jewelry. At times, her anger overcame her practicality, and the urge to smash and destroy arose, but she managed to control it. Despite the strange lack of photos and personal effects like marriage certificates and tax forms, she reminded herself that the objects told stories. Ruby red must have been her mother's favorite color, there was so much of it. She must have gone to scores of elegant events, because she had a closet full of evening gowns and sparkly things. She hadn't liked to cook, for the kitchen held few implements and the refrigerator contained mostly frozen TV dinners.

Going through the CDs, she found only Spanish Flamen-co and Latin dance music. Josephine imagined her mother holding dance parties, to which she was never invited, and let the hurt wash over her for a few minutes, then suppressed her feelings yet again. She could have easily smashed those recordings into bits, but instead she sold them.

AUGUST ARRIVED, HUMID and hot. Determined to finish cleaning out the house before school started, Josephine donned her dust mask. She pulled down hard on the latch to the attic stairs and lifted her feet to give it her whole weight. It slowly creaked open, the stairs descending in a cloud of dust. Her eyes watered and burned but she pulled the latex gloves out of her pocket and climbed through the opening.

A single room ran the length of the house. Weak light filtered into the space through small windows. Cobwebs covered open beams under a slanted roof. Their silvery threads drooped so low they almost touched the floor in places. She flicked the light switch. Bare bulbs attached to the beams illuminated boxes and furniture piled to the height of her chin all the way across the attic.

She opened the closest box. It held plastic Christmas ornaments. She dropped it down the stairs before opening another box. More ornaments. By lunchtime, she'd cleared a five foot space around the attic entrance and hauled everything to her sorting area in the dining room. She was dripping wet inside her yellow coveralls. Dust and spider webs clung to her sweaty face and hair. She showered, drank half a liter of water, downed a sandwich, and suited up again.

Late in the day, she lifted up an armful of sun-rotted drapes, and was so surprised to discover her grandmother's old chest underneath them that she fell on her butt. Collecting herself, she ran her hands over the familiar old wood trunk with its leather and brass fittings.

Suddenly she was a child again:

SHE WAS WITH her cousins in an attic smaller than this one. Regina stood next to her while she lifted the chest's lid. When the boys snuck up on them with plastic swords and pounced, all of the cousins dissolved into giggles. Once they calmed down, they pulled out the toy cars, Legos, teddy bears, and dolls Grandmother Rose kept in the trunk's spacious interior. The others started playing, but Josephine opened the compartment in the trunk's wall. Their grandmother always hid candies and pennies in it for them. She pulled out a handful and handed half to Regina. The boys punched them, trying to get all the treats. She and Regina fought them off until their grandmother trudged up the stairs and told them to stop fighting and share.

How many times had something like that happened when she was a little girl? Her cousins had lived nearby; their family hadn't moved to Seattle until after Grandmother's death.

With a sigh, Josephine dropped her head on the chest, hoping to catch a little of the jasmine scent Grandmother Rose used to wear, and feel again her grandmother's kindness and love. She imagined burying herself in the old woman's arms. If she could only bring her back to life, she would stop being so lonely and upset. But that, of course, was impossible.

The lid lifted easily, its leather hinges still intact. Velvet skirts covered in beads and mirrors filled the top tray. Again, she was a child. Her mother walked in the front door at Grandmother Rose's in one of these outfits, her arms loaded with presents. Josephine ran to her, and she swung her around and around. Then Josephine ripped the paper off one of the presents to reveal a baby doll in a pink dress with a matching hair bow, exactly liked she'd wanted. She squealed and hugged her mother.

Her mother hadn't stayed long, maybe a few days. After her mother left, Grandmother Rose held her while she cried herself to sleep. How many times had that happened before she'd learned not to get excited when her mother visited? The last time, the day of Rose's funeral, she'd seen her mother park in front of the house, and gone into her room and closed the door.

Josephine shook herself and slid the skirts into a clean garbage bag. The wooden tray lifted out easily to reveal a pile of gaudy jewelry and scarves, which she added to the bag. Some vintage store would love the old clothes; she certainly didn't want them. She lifted out another tray and inhaled sharply. There lay what she'd hoped to find: photo albums. She set the stack off to the side, not quite ready to face their contents, and finished emptying the bottom of the trunk of a few worn-out slippers, high-heeled dance shoes, and some peasant blouses. Then she reached into the pocket in the lid and pulled out a thick envelope which rustled a little, as if filled with confetti. It went on top of the albums.

Her hands shook as she ran them around the inside wall of the trunk. When she found the right spot, she pushed gently and a latch released. A thin piece of wood swung outward to reveal a hole in the side of the trunk. She reached inside. Her fingers closed around the end of a box. As soon as she felt it, she knew exactly what it was.

She raced down the stairs to take the familiar red velvet case into the bright kitchen. The box, worn and shiny from years of handling, brought back a wealth of memories. Setting it on the counter, she carefully pulled up the filigreed latch and opened the case. Her grandmother's necklace sparkled at her.

Lifting it to the sunlight streaming through the windows, she marveled at its beauty. A lacy gold cross held diamonds and rubies. More gems sparkled along the chain. She stripped off her filthy coveralls, wrapped the necklace around her neck and walked up the stairs to the master bedroom where she could examine herself in her mother's antique mirror.

Even though she wore an old tank top, the red, white and

gold of the necklace transformed her into a queen, the stones complementing her dark hair and olive skin. No wonder Grandmother Rose had worn it every day.

Josephine sank onto the bed. She closed her eyes, remembering the moment when she'd been exiled for good.

AFTER HER GRANDMOTHER'S death, she and her mother had moved into a small apartment together, not far from here, in downtown Pittsburgh. Her mother had spoiled her, and Josephine had gradually stopped crying all the time and begun to feel at ease with this mother she barely knew.

A month later, her mother walked out of her bedroom, wearing Grandmother Rose's necklace. Josephine flew at her, screaming and scratching at her like a rabid raccoon, trying to remove it. "That's not yours," she screamed. "It's Aunt Lillian's. You have no right to it!" All of the years of upset came tumbling out of her until her voice failed.

Her mother pushed her away. "You brat. Go to your room. Now. I will not have this."

Josephine spit at her and stomped off, fuming because Grandmother Rose had promised the necklace to Aunt Lillian, a much nicer person than her own mother. Through the thin door, she heard her mother on the phone. "I can't handle her. I'm not cut out for this," she shouted. Josephine covered her head with a pillow. She didn't want to hear the rest.

The next day, her mother came into Josephine's room, carrying a suitcase. "Pack this with everything you'll need for the summer."

"Why?"

"We're leaving in half an hour." She turned on her heels and clicked away down the hallway.

Josephine did her best to figure out what to take. When her mother returned, she snapped the suitcase closed, handed Josephine her sweater, picked up the luggage, and carried it to the car, all without saying a word.

"Where are we going?" Josephine asked over and over as they drove to the airport.

Her mother looked straight ahead at the road, her lips tight. "You're going to your paternal grandparents." She said very little else, as they parked and her mother led her into the terminal, got her checked in, and said goodbye. Her final words were: "Behave yourself."

When Josephine came out of the gate with the stewardess, she noticed two stern-looking, thin, grey-haired people and prayed they would not be her grandparents, but they were. "Welcome to Des Moines," they said, but their tone was dry and sharp, as if they'd rather she hadn't come.

She stared at them, tying to find the father she didn't remember in their faces.

"Why are you examining us?" her grandmother said, sharply. "Let's go."

"Will you tell me about my father?" Josephine asked as they walked to the luggage carousel.

"No, we won't. It was sinful and selfish for him to take his own life, instead of facing his troubles like a man. Never speak of him again."

Josephine felt something die inside her. She walked quietly next to them down the tarmac, trying to stay as far away from these harsh people as she could.

At breakfast the next morning, lumpy oatmeal as she recalled, her grandmother laid down a set of rules: no television, no speaking to adults unless they spoke to you first, no laughing, no pants, skirts must end below the knee, she must attend Sunday Mass and avoid associating with any other children. She shrunk into herself, lying on her bed most of the day, reading, or staring at the ceiling, inventing an adventure-filled life with her mother.

At the end of the summer, her grandparents drove her to

St. Catherine's Boarding School for Girls and left her there.
At first, she hated the school almost as much as their home.
Slowly, though, she adapted and discovered she could escape
her feelings by studying hard. The nuns were strict but kind.
She did her best to please them, so she wouldn't be sent back
to those horrid grandparents.

At Christmas, her mother arrived, bearing an armload
of gifts and whisking her off to a hotel for a few days. She
left, promising to return for her birthday in April. Another
broken promise, Josephine recalled bitterly. She hadn't seen
her mother again until the end of that summer, when her
grandparents dropped her off early at school, and her mother took her on a driving trip. Josephine remembered wasting
those few precious days explaining why she didn't want to
spend another summer with her grandparents.

"They don't want you back, anyway," her mother had
said. "It's too hard on them."

Josephine had been relieved. She'd stayed at the school
year-round, spending two weeks every summer in Seattle
with Aunt Lillian, Uncle Alan and their five children.

She could count on one hand the number of times she'd
seen her mother after that.

When her mother did visit, she swept into the dorm,

packed a suitcase for her daughter, and took Josephine out of her classes. Once, they went to Disney World. Another time, they visited Washington, DC and spent their days visiting museums.

JOSEPHINE SHOOK HERSELF. She'd been sitting on the bed for over an hour. All those memories, yet she was no closer to understanding her mother than she'd ever been.

Hoping they held some answers, she retrieved the envelope and albums from the attic and took them to the antique maple table in the dining room. Opening the envelope, she discovered the reason for the rustling; it was full of newspaper clippings.

The top article was a brief announcement for a dance performance:

Flamenco at the Main Street Theater

World-renowned flamenco dancer Theresa Fondant will appear on

Thursday, June 15th, along with her troupe and the amazing Geraldo Marcatto on guitar. Don't miss this exciting opportunity to see authentic dances from the Andalusia region of Spain.

Josephine stared in shock at the press release. What was this about flamenco and world-famous? She flipped through the clippings. Most were in foreign languages: Spanish, Italian, something which looked Slavic. She couldn't read them, but her mother's name jumped out at her from each article, often with a photograph of her mother in an exotic costume, her hands posed upwards, in a flourish. This certainly explained the empty room with the stereo system.

Why didn't I know about this? How come no one told me? Or did they, and I didn't listen?

No, Josephine realized, she had known, but she'd been too hurt and angry to accept that her mother loved dance more than she loved her, so she'd pretended it wasn't true, and made up ugly stories to take the place of the reality that her mother didn't have time for her. It all came back, the way her mother would say that she had to leave, or her aunt would say that her mother couldn't visit, because she had a performance, a rehearsal, or even a workshop. "I'm flying to Spain tomorrow." Or Portugal, New York City, or any place but where Josephine waited in vain for a glimpse of the famous Theresa Fondant. And of course, the other girls at the school noticed her mother's absence and ragged her constantly. No wonder she'd turned to her books, finding comfort in the certainty of numbers and formulas.

Shaken, she examined the albums. The one on top held her baby pictures, her parents and grandparents wreathed in big smiles with her in their arms. In the next album, she grew older on each page, and her parents' smiles more forced. There was a photo of her and her mother in black dresses and small black hats at her father's funeral. She stared at that page a long time, but she couldn't bring up even a fleeting image of the day, or of the father who had shot himself before she turned four. It seemed odd that she didn't remember him. A little numb, she opened the third album. She stopped at a photo from her grandmother's funeral and traced the sad faces. The rest of the book was blank, the plastic slots untouched. Her heart ached. Her mother had not cared enough to record those years.

Only the very last page held anything: a collage of photos from her high school graduation. Someone must have sent them to her mother, who hadn't bothered to attend. The ache turned to bitterness. What had been wrong with her goddamn mother that she hadn't even called to congratulate her and wish her good luck?

Upset, she took a break and went outside. Over the past two months, she'd dug out the weeds and trimmed the bushes. Before the house went up for sale, she planned to put in some flowers, but it was too hot to work on the yard. Instead, she walked around the neighborhood, admiring tidy lawns and well-kept houses. Breathing deeply, she went back inside, poured herself a cup of cold coffee and returned to the albums.

The next one was dedicated to her father, with a florid inscription in the front, many photos of him, articles about his suicide, and pressed flowers from his memorial service. Her mother must have loved him, given this tribute. Josephine closed her eyes, trying once again to conjure him from the past, but the man in the photos remained a stranger.

The last book held the letters she'd written her mother from the time she went to board at St. Catherine's, to the time when she'd given up and stopped writing. There were the photos she'd sent from her college graduation, her first time skiing, and her first dog. Something fell out on the floor. She leaned over and picked it up. It was a half-written letter to her from her mother, dated a week before Josephine had received her MS in Physics:

Dear Josephine,

Congratulations. I am so proud of you, even though I have had little part in your life. Forgive me

Then it stopped, as if her mother didn't know what to say. Josephine felt numb. She couldn't fit the idea that her mother had given a shit into the story she'd told herself all her life.

A WEEK LATER, Josephine drove home to Cleveland to prep for the school year. On Friday night, she donned the necklace and examined herself in her bathroom mirror. She resembled her mother, with the same green eyes, the same dark curls, the same long nose with a bump in the middle. Her chin was softer, but still protruded forward. Seeing her reflection reminded her that she couldn't in good conscience keep the heirloom—it belonged to her aunt.

Why haven't you asked your aunt about your mother?

I was afraid.

Of what? Of the truth?

Yes. Of finding out she never loved me, that I behaved so badly she gave up on me.

You're not a child anymore. Do you really still believe that?

Maybe.

I doubt it's true, but it's time to find out. Call Aunt Lillian.

THE SECOND WEEKEND in October, Josephine flew to Seattle. Lillian's wrinkled face broke into a wide smile when she opened the door. "Come in, dear. You can hang your coat in the closet and put your suitcase in the guest room. It's down the hall to your right. I'm fixing dinner. It's almost ready."

Josephine settled herself in the bedroom, slipped the necklace box out of her suitcase, and followed the scent of roast chicken to the kitchen.

Her aunt stood over the stove, her face intent on something in a pan. "Do you mind setting the table, dear?"

"Of course not."

"Use the good china. It's in the buffet," her aunt said.

Josephine walked through the door to the dining area, which was divided from the kitchen by a long, chest-high counter. She hid the box behind a vase on the old-fashioned buffet, then busied herself getting out the china, crystal water glasses, and silver cutlery. She lifted a silver candle holder down from the buffet and drew two cloth napkins out of one of its drawers. Once the table was set, she leaned over the counter. "How are my cousins?" she asked.

"Regina is getting married again."

"To whom?" Josephine had been so out of touch, she didn't even know Regina had gotten divorced.

"A man from one of her college classes. He popped the question last week. The kids seem to like him."

"That's exciting."

"Yes, I am pleased." Her aunt plopped on a chair and set her feet on her kitchen stool.

For the first time, it occurred to Josephine that her aunt was no longer young. "How are you feeling?"

"As good as can be expected at sixty-seven. My ankles swell. The doctor says to put my feet up in the evenings."

"You're grinning. Is the doctor cute?"

Her aunt dismissed the idea, with a swipe of her hand in front of her face and a quick turn of her head. She laughed. "He's about fifteen."

"Auntie! You have a crush on him!"

"Everyone does," Lillian answered, just as the oven timer dinged. "Bring the salad and the mashed potatoes." Lillian removed the chicken from the oven and slipped it onto a serving platter.

They carried their food into the dining room, said a quick grace, and started eating.

"How long are you staying?" Lillian asked.

"Until Sunday. I have to teach Monday morning."

"That's all? It's an awfully long flight for such a short stay.

What's so important that it couldn't wait until you had more time?"

Josephine stood up and retrieved the box. "This."

Lillian's mouth tightened. She wiped her face with her napkin. She stood up abruptly and picked up her plate. "Almost time for my show. We'll talk in the morning. You finish your meal."

AFTER BREAKFAST THE next morning, Lillian pointed to the box. "Bring that into the living room."

Josephine followed her down the hall and settled on the couch with the necklace in her lap. She tapped it. "I believe this is yours."

"No, honey. It belongs to you."

"But Grandmother Rose wanted you to have it. I was so mad when I saw that Mom had it."

"I know. She called me. She didn't know what to do to calm you down so you could listen to her explanation."

"So she sent me to my grandparents instead?" Josephine's voice rose. She clenched her fists.

Lillian sighed. "That isn't why she sent you there."

Josephine glared at her aunt. "Like hell she didn't. You should have seen her face at the airport the next day. She would hardly speak to me." She stomped out of the room, and went into the bathroom. Running water on her face, she willed herself to calm down and control her emotions. After drying off, she took another deep breath, returned to the living room and apologized.

"It's okay. I understand this is difficult. But listen to what I have to say."

Josephine picked up the necklace box and walked across the room to the television. She reminded herself that she was here to learn the truth, even if it hurt. "Did she need the money? I had it appraised. It's valuable."

Lillian sighed and leaned back. "It had nothing to do with money. Theresa always loved the necklace, from the time she was a little girl. So, after Mama died, I gave it to her."

"Didn't you—don't you—want it?"

Lillian shook her head. "Not really." She patted the couch. "Sit, child. You make me nervous."

Once Josephine obeyed, her aunt continued. "For one thing, that necklace is too ornate for my taste. But, more importantly, it's connected to our gypsy past, and I didn't want to believe the stories about our gypsy ancestors. Your mother, on the other hand, loved the idea. She looked like a gypsy, and she wanted to become one. She begged our uncles to tell us about our ancestors over and over."

"What stories?" Josephine settled into the corner of the couch and let her hands relax.

"According to legend, one of our first ancestors was a gitano, an Andalusian gypsy, named Eduardo."

"Spanish?"

Lillian nodded. "His wife, Collette, was French."

"And?"

"Legend has it that Colette met Eduardo while she was visiting a friend in Seville for the summer. He was a gypsy, so it's difficult to believe they would have ever come in contact, but supposedly they did. He seduced her with his good looks and charm and they fell deeply in love. So much so, that they came up with a plan to end up together. She told him the route her coach would take when she left for Paris, and he and his brothers waited on a lonely stretch of road near Marseille to attack it. They held a knife to her coachman's throat and tied up Collette and her maid. Eduardo plucked the necklace right off Colette's neck and took a bag of gold."

"Wow."

"When soldiers found Collette and her entourage, they chased after the thieves, but the brothers had too much of a head start. They secured passage from Marseilles to America and rode their horses right onto the ship and into the hold. The ship set sail. The soldiers arrived at the dock soon after. They fired warning shots, but the captain refused to turn back."

"You mean this might be true? I always thought Uncle Marcel made up tales about swordsmen and bandits to entertain us kids!"

"Who knows? It was such a long time ago. I suspect the details have been elaborated a great deal. Colette's wealthy husband tried to have the brothers arrested after they arrived in New York, but they eluded capture. Colette came to Boston two years later, to visit friends, and never went back to France. Right before she was to return, she met up with Eduardo and vanished with him into the wilds of Ohio."

Josephine thought about the traffic she faced every day on her way to work. Those 'wilds' were long gone, themselves the stuff of legends. She turned the tale over in her mind, enjoying the possibility that she had such dashing ancestors. Still, it didn't quite make sense. "This seems so cloak and dagger. Why didn't she come with Eduardo in the first place?"

"They thought it was too dangerous. If he was captured

or killed, she could claim she was relieved he was no longer a threat, and go on with life as usual."

"All very romantic."

"Your mother thought so. I find the idea embarrassing. I'd rather have well-behaved ancestors. Here, hand me that box," her aunt said.

Josephine reached across the gap between them.

Lillian opened the clasp and lifted the necklace to the light. "It's beautiful, isn't it? Your mother loved it so much she couldn't bear to lose it, so she hid it in the old trunk. She figured that if something happened to her, you'd find it there. She wanted you to have it."

Josephine made a strangled noise.

"I know this isn't easy, child, but you should know about her. She was obsessed with our heritage. She learned everything she could about it. She wore flowing scarves and long colorful skirts and pretended to tell fortunes. She talked Papa into flamenco classes. Eventually flamenco became her whole world. She traveled constantly, and danced long hours."

"Why did she have me, then?"

"She—oh dear, how do I say this?" Lillian patted Josephine's knee. "Your mother wanted you, more than anything. She loved you, no matter what you might think."

"But she loved dance more."

Lillian turned back to her, tears in her eyes. "You don't know that. She let others raise you because she couldn't cope. If you cried, she broke out in hysterics. If you had a scraped knee, she fainted. If you were angry, and all children get angry, she'd go in her room and hide. I didn't understand it, but we urged her to let Mama raise you after your father's death."

"And after Grandmama Rose died, why didn't you take me?"

"We couldn't. We already had our five, and we could barely manage them."

Some belligerent childishness rose in Josephine. She pointed at the necklace. "She sent me to those awful people because I had a tantrum over that."

"No, honey." Lillian held it up again. "No, they'd already agreed to take you. In fact, it was their idea. They thought your gypsy relatives had let you run wild for too long. You needed a home with simple rules and a regular schedule."

"How do you know all that?"

"Your mother talked it over with me. I thought they were right, but, by the end of the summer, you'd withdrawn into a shell. They worried the transition had been too difficult."

"They did? I thought they hated me."

"Oh, child, how could anyone hate you? No, they were old and set in their ways, that's all. Anyway, we discussed what to do, and decided to try boarding school."

"It was certainly better than their home."

"Each time Theresa visited, you were happier and more integrated into the school. I saw that, too, when you visited us."

Josephine sighed. This was too much to absorb. "I need some time alone."

"If it isn't raining, you should walk down to the park. It's just four blocks to the west. Take an umbrella out of the hall closet, just in case."

A light drizzle greeted Josephine when she exited the building. The mistiness of it struck her as perfect for such an intense day. Perhaps the rain would wash away her misconceptions about her childhood, and all the anger and hurt she'd nursed for a zillion years. She found the park and kept going until her aunt's words started to make sense. Then she turned around, ready to ask more questions.

She waited until Lillian served afternoon tea, with a plate of pastries. They were at the dining room table, using a china tea set with a delicate rose pattern. Lillian, Josephine noticed, liked elegant things and everything in its proper place, even nieces.

But Josephine didn't want to fit into the china cabinet. She wanted to shock her aunt with her pain, to call her out for glossing over the ugly reality that morning. "If my mother loved me so damn much," she spat, "why did she stop visiting? Why didn't I ever see her again?"

Lillian set her cup in its saucer and regarded her niece. "When was that?"

"I never saw her after my sophomore year of high school."

"Oh, child," her aunt said, looking concerned. "I didn't know. Why didn't you say something to me?"

"How could I? I thought something was so terribly wrong with me that even my own mother wouldn't visit me. If I asked you and you told me the truth, how could I have lived with myself?"

"Oh, child. I wish you'd asked me this a long time ago. You could have saved yourself a lot of grief."

Josephine closed her eyes, reliving the embarrassment and hurt of her teen years, feelings which had followed her into the present.

Her aunt pulled her chair around next to hers and hugged her. "There wasn't anything wrong with you, sweetheart."

"I tried so hard to become someone she could love." Josephine began crying, hard. Her aunt sat with her, pulling her close, until the tears slowed.

"It wasn't your fault. Theresa—well, she never could deal with her mistakes. She'd failed you, and she knew it."

"She never even wrote," Josephine stammered. "I wrote and wrote and she never answered."

Lillian patted her back and waited until the tears slowed. "You never told me. I thought you two had grown closer over the years."

"I lied." She dropped her head onto her hands. "I made it all up."

Lillian pushed Josephine's tea cup and saucer into the center of the table. "I would have, too, in those circumstances. Come, I have something to show you."

Josephine stumbled to her feet and followed her aunt to her sewing room. Lillian reached into a bookshelf and pulled out a photo album. She took it to the living room, and sat next to Josephine on the couch.

"Your mother wasn't much of a correspondent, but we

saw each other every couple of years, sometimes in Pittsburgh or here, but more often in Spain. She spent six months out of the year there, and probably only two in that house she left you. I want you to see these pictures, and hear her story."

"You said she died in Spain when you called."

"Yes. In a dreadful auto accident. An oncoming driver fell asleep and smashed into the front of her car. She and her husband died instantly."

"What husband?"

"Let me tell you." For the next few hours, they looked at pictures of Theresa, and Lillian told her about her mother. When she finished talking, Josephine felt as if an enormous load had been lifted off her heart. She could never forgive her mother for abandoning her to the care of others, but at least her mother no longer felt like a complete stranger.

THE NEXT MORNING, while Josephine packed her carry-on, Lillian came into the room.

"Don't forget this," she held out the box with the necklace.

Josephine pushed it away. "You should give it to Regina when she gets married."

"She won't want it. Besides, Colette gave it to her oldest daughter when she married, and she gave it to her oldest on her wedding day. If Mama had kept to family tradition, she would have given it to your mother, but she loved it too much to pass it on. So it's yours."

"I've never married." Her anger and sadness had driven away every man she'd dated. A faint hope arose that she could change that now.

"That doesn't mean you never will. Before that, though, it would help if you spent more time with relatives and friends and learned how to be close to other people. Obviously, you're used to keeping to yourself."

Josephine's mouth opened, ready to protest, but then she closed it. Her aunt was right.

Lillian smiled. "The whole family is coming for Christmas. Please join us. You can stay with Regina, I already asked her."

A wave of something undefinable washed over Josephine, bringing a sense that she belonged, that she was wanted, perhaps even loved. "Yes," she said, and smiled so hard her face ached. "I'll come."

"Perhaps while you're here, I'll introduce you to my doctor. He's single."

Josephine raised her eyebrows. "Isn't he a little young for an old maid in her forties?"

"Not at all, dear. I joke that anyone under sixty looks like a kid to me. He went to school with Regina, so he is a year younger than you. I shall invite him to dinner."

"You're kidding?"

"Actually, no. You'll adore him."

THE AFFAIR

GEORGE WAS CERTAIN his wife was having an affair. She glowed in a way which spoke of only one thing: sex. And it certainly wasn't sex with him. After fourteen years, their romantic life consisted of a quick kiss in the morning, another right before bed, and dutiful intercourse the last Friday of every month.

She'd grown slowly more radiant ever since she'd taken that writing workshop in the summer, or had it been painting? No, maybe it was quilting. She was always going to something; he couldn't keep track. She must have hooked up with another creative sort, but he hadn't asked her about it, of course he hadn't. What if she told the truth? Would that end their marriage?

And what if she lied? He didn't want to see the quick

shift of her eyes to the right, the way they always did when she tried to pretend she hadn't cheated on her diet, or hadn't spent too much money on shoes.

Instead, George peeked at her cell phone every time she left it lying around. Once he even called a number that appeared frequently, but, when her best friend answered, he hung up. And, darn it, his wife never said anything suspicious when he eavesdropped. He even cracked her email password, although he was too timid to actually read her email.

All of his spying turned up nothing. He'd never before realized what a master of deceit he'd married.

Finally, George could stand the upwelling of jealousy no longer. He took a vacation day without telling her. Instead of going to work, he sat in a coffee shop and watched the first snow of the winter dust the trees. Once he was certain she had left for her job at the bank, he returned home and began searching the house. If she was cheating on him, he would surely find some trace of it.

He examined everything in her purses and coat pockets, being careful to leave the contents exactly as he found them. Nothing.

Sweat beaded his face. His shirt was dark around the

armpits. Shame made him slow his search. Perhaps his wife was innocent, and he was the guilty one for doubting her. But then he remembered the song she'd sung under her breath last night and forced himself to continue. She never sang unless the radio was playing.

Her dresser drawers and closet didn't yield anything suspicious. Perhaps she kept new clothes at her lover's place. He turned green at the thought of her in a sexy negligee, a gift from this unknown quilter/painter/writer.

It was only noon, but his stomach threatened to rebel and he felt like he'd been at his spying for weeks. Still, her project room was the most likely place for evidence, so he entered it and looked around.

Her easel sat in the corner, covered with dust. There was nothing in the sewing box, or hidden under her stash of old buttons. Perhaps, George considered, she hid love notes inside a book. He started to pull out one whose worn cover seemed suspicious, but he saw a shoebox on the top of the bookshelf, and lifted it down instead.

Inside, packed tightly together, index cards and miscellaneous bits of paper mocked him. His feeling of triumph was accompanied by a sinking sensation in his stomach. He hauled his find to his office.

For over an hour, he sat at his desk, unsure whether he dared read the love notes. But he had to, didn't he? He owed himself that much. Finally, he poured himself a drink from the bottle of scotch he hid in his safe and took the glass to his desk. He sipped, then read the first card.

Emily is thirteen, with black eyes and long straight black hair. She's vivacious, loves horses and has two younger sisters.

"Huh?" he said, out loud.

The next card was even more puzzling. It described Emily's mother and their cat.

More cards described people, then there were a few colored cards devoted to what Emily wanted and what stood in her way.

George flipped on through the box. Everything was in his wife's handwriting. No love notes.

Making sure to place each item exactly as he'd found it, he returned everything to the box. As he replaced it on top of the bookshelf, he saw a suspicious-looking notebook that he hadn't noticed before. He took it down and sat at his wife's desk, reading bits here and there, about Emily, a teenaged detective, on the trail of a robber. How odd that his wife hadn't said a word to him about this project, but, then again, he usually dismissed her creative pursuits.

Bile rose in George's throat. Searching her things was fruitless. He had to do the unthinkable and read her emails. He started towards her computer, but the fading light caused him to glance at his watch. Three-thirty. He didn't know what time she got off work. She was always home when he arrived a little after six. He'd better get out of here.

Back at the café, with his laptop open and her email in front of him, he didn't hesitate to open one from her sister. *So glad you've found your passion. I can't wait to read it. Give George my love.*

Wait, 'passion' and 'read it' didn't fit together. This must be some kind of code. He dug deeper. More emails talked about her novel, and how deeply satisfied she felt when she was inventing her story. *I feel ten years younger,* she wrote. *I wish George would notice.*

He blushed deeply, shame washing over him. Of course he'd noticed, but he'd been a scared, jealous fool, acting like a teenager. That evening, he would ask her why she was so happy. Perhaps she would confess to the novel and his agony could end. And from now on, he swore, he would take more interest in her life.

FADED JEANS

ALL PATRICIA COULD see as she peered into the hallway through the small glass window in her office door was a row of knees in faded blue jeans and work pants. She sighed. She'd grown up in this small rural community. She knew many of the people who'd come today. She'd gone to high school with a couple of them; half of them attended her church. They'd always worked hard and taken good care of their children. The housing crash that had led to this recession wasn't their fault. It was horrible that she only had one small job to give out today, one poorly paid position for some desperate person with a household of dependents.

She clicked her tongue and sat at her computer to scan the files once more. The work center required her to pick the most qualified candidate for each job, but something had broken inside her this morning when she realized the situation. She just couldn't bring herself to tell all but one person to go home, not that many of them had homes to go to anymore.

Still she had to select someone, or else she'd lose her job, and her children would be the ones without a roof over their heads. Their father had left town two months ago, after the farm equipment place laid him off. He'd hoped there would be more opportunities in a larger city, but so far all he'd found was a minimum wage position doing part-time maintenance for a hotel. She looked over at the photo of him and their three kids next to her monitor and made up her mind to choose the person with the most children, one whose spouse was also unemployed. If her family was in need, she'd hope someone would help them out, wouldn't she? Silly, she supposed, but how else was she supposed to decide? Who needed any qualifications to post signs on foreclosed homes?

Biting her lip, she chose a man with five kids under the age of ten. He'd do. Please God, tomorrow would be a better day, and there'd be more jobs, good paying ones, to hand out.

As soon as she opened the door, all of the people stood, their desperate eyes searching her face, and she wanted to cry. Their clothes hung off of them, especially the men, men who had once been strong ranch hands and construction workers, perhaps even ranch owners and contractors. Many of them stank, from living out of their cars or in tents on BLM land. Each morning they came here, with hope in their hearts, and each morning she sent more of them away, jobless.

It was awful, and now all she had was one measly assignment, pasting signs on homes they perhaps used to own.

"Mark Nolan," she said, the name catching in her throat. "The rest of you can leave."

All but one head dropped and they shuffled away. Mr. Nolan patted each of their backs as they left. Once they were gone, she told him where to meet his temporary employer, then she went into her office, locked the door, and stared at the screen for a long time, not seeing a thing.

COLUMNS

THE ROAR OF the garage door opening and closing woke Lacy from her nap. Her father must be home from his law office. She supposed that she should get up and go downstairs to greet him, but they still had plenty of time together before she headed back to college for the spring term. Having talked herself out of getting up, she snuggled deeper into the familiar softness of her bed, giving in to the stupor induced by the warm spring day, the perfume of her mother's lilacs, and the exhaustion she felt after final exams.

She had almost dozed off again when the clack of the front door latch and the screech of the porch swing brought her back to full awareness. Her parent's voices rose through her open window, first her mother's sharp tones, then her father's low rumble.

As always, the porch roof muffled their words, but she thought her father said her name. Curious why they were talking about her, she stretched and yawned, then stood. Leaving on the old shorts and tank top she'd slept in, she ran her fingers through her matted long, dark-blond hair, tied it into a bun, set her black-rimmed glasses on her nose, and pulled on her running shoes. Carefully, she tiptoed down the wide front staircase towards the entry foyer.

Her parents had propped the front doors wide open to let in the early evening breeze, and closed the screen doors against bugs. Ice cubes rattled against the sides of their glasses. They were arguing, their voices too low for her to catch their sentences over the chirping of birds conversing about nest-building.

A better child would join her parents on the porch, and ask what they were talking about, but Lacy had learned a long time ago that they would switch to gossip or the weather the minute they heard or saw her. She slipped down the hallway, out the back door, and around the house to the side of the old-fashioned porch, where she stationed herself behind one of the four stately Corinthian columns which held up the porch roof. A large flower box filled with gardenias ran between the back column and the front one. Kneeling and crawling forward from her hiding place, she peered through the gap between the flower box and the column, verified that her parents were settled in their seats with their glasses, and sat out of sight with her back half against the column and half against the house.

The ground, cool and damp from yesterday's rain, felt good, even though she could already sense the water soaking through her shorts. They'd have grass stains on them, but they were old, and already stained.

She'd first hidden here when she was nine. They'd just moved into this stately old house, and her parents were enjoying the novelty of sitting in the shade of the porch, sipping lemonade. She hadn't meant to listen that day; she'd been exploring the yard when she heard their voices and crept closer and closer, until her ears were pressed against the crack. Her parents never knew she'd heard every word. As she grew older, she'd discovered that they felt free to talk about their problems out here, and her eavesdropping had become a habit.

When she was young, she'd been careless. Interested in some discussion about her brothers, she'd creep forward to hear more, and even poke her head out over the top of the flowers. Her parents would catch her, and punish her severely. Eventually, she'd learned to sit back out of sight, and hold very, very still. From this spot, she could usually hear most of their conversation.

She hadn't been caught since she was twelve, so she relaxed in her hiding place. Her father's low rumbling reassured her that they weren't really arguing, until her mother interrupted him:

"Do not stand up for her, Harold."

Lacy sat taller and inched over, almost to the edge of the column.

Her father sighed and the swing creaked. "I keep telling you. The world has changed."

"I know that. I'm not stupid."

"You're your father's daughter. There's no getting around it."

"So? He brought me up right. A woman's place is in the home, not in some physics laboratory."

Oh, so that's it. She must have opened my mail. I come by my snooping honestly, don't I?

"You're behind the times, Maggie."

"What does that mean?"

"Families need two incomes. Women need a profession. They don't go to college to become a Mrs. anymore."

"Is that what you think I did?" Her mother's voice was loud and angry.

Her father stood and paced, as if gathering his thoughts or trying to control his irritation at her mother. He often walked back and forth when he was troubled. At one point, his footsteps came so close that the edge of his jacket almost touched Lacy. She wondered if he'd seen her, but he didn't say anything; he simply turned and kept pacing. After awhile, the swing screeched under his weight, covering his retort just enough that she couldn't pick out the words.

"So what if I did?" her mother asked. "We all did in those days. I realize Lacy needs an education. It's just her choice of major that upsets me."

Lacy balled up her fists, as if ready to punch her mother. *Physics is interesting.*

"She's smart enough."

"I don't doubt it. But do you really want your daughter working with a bunch of nerdy guys?"

"I will not tell her we will only support her if she studies something you consider appropriate for a woman."

"She'll find out the hard way, then." Her mother's voice was tight and angry. There was a scraping sound, then her mother's heels tapped across the porch to the screen door, which opened and closed behind her.

Lacy had had enough. She didn't care what punishment her parents imposed for eavesdropping. She stood and marched around to the front of the steps and up onto the porch. Eyes blazing, she confronted her father. "She has no right to control my future. How dare you let her?"

She started towards the door, but her father's voice stopped her. "Let's go for a walk."

Lacy gazed across the expanse of grass in front of the house to the pond at the far side, and the thin fringe of trees which separated their property from the lane beyond. "She wants me to get married to some rich guy and have his babies."

"You don't understand."

"I don't?" Suddenly, she felt an awful sensation in her chest, as if she was being filled with burning embers. "What about my dreams? Doesn't she care if I'm happy?" Desperate to escape, she raced down the steps and out onto the lawn, towards the pond.

"Lacy," her father shouted.

Before she reached the edge of the lawn, she doubled over, crying. After a few seconds, a hand landed gently on her back. "Come on," her father said. "Get it out, then let's walk."

She took a few deep breaths, shook off his hand, and headed towards the pond, then through the woods to the lane. She turned towards the end, a half mile away.

"Feel better?" he asked, pulling up next to her and matching her stride. He'd taken off the jacket he wore to the office and left it somewhere, probably on a tree branch. As they walked, he rolled up his sleeves and removed his tie, stuffing it in his pants pocket.

"A little. But why is Mama being so awful? I thought she was proud of me."

"She is, honey. She's just letting her fears get the best of her."

Lacy shook her head, not understanding.

"She sees things on the news, about rape on campus, or women making less than men for the same jobs, and she worries. That's all."

She absorbed his words, but it didn't explain her mother's refusal to let her major in science. "It's more than that. She buys all that conservative crap about women kowtowing to men."

Lacy, realizing that he wasn't with her anymore, turned and came back to where he stood, glaring at her, his face white and angry, his jaw tight. Beads of sweat dripped out of his short-cropped blond hair, and rolled down his round face. He took off his glasses, wiped off his face with his handker-chief, and replaced the spectacles.

"What?" she asked.

"Don't ever put your mother down. She gave her heart and soul to raising you kids and making a home for us."

Her heart softened a little. It was sweet, the way he loved her mother. His words made her feel guilty, bring back all the times her mother had driven her places, and the way she'd patched up her knees with a kiss, or mended the rips in her clothes. "Sorry. I didn't mean to sound ungrateful." *Although she sure could have encouraged me to take more math and science in high school.* Lacy knew better than to articulate that thought.

He started walking again, faster than before, and Lacy struggled to keep up with his longer strides.

"Your mother," he said, out of the side of his mouth, "did what she wanted."

Nearly out of breath trying to keep up, Lacy panted, her words coming out a few at a time. "I didn't mean to say what she chose is wrong. It's what all of her friends did, too, so that's the world she knows. But I want a different life."

Her father's face softened, and his steps slowed to a more

reasonable pace. "I know. And I support you."

"Are you going to pay for it, or will I have to get a job?" She'd always assumed there was plenty of money in her college fund, but now she wondered.

"You need to talk to your mother."

"But it's your money. You earn it."

His face grew hard, and he stared ahead as if he had encountered something distasteful. "No. It's *our* money. You think you're a modern girl, but that's a very un-modern statement. Sure, I practice law, but I couldn't if she didn't do everything else. We are a team. We make decisions together. She's the one you need to convince. Not me."

Lacy bit her lip. "She always avoids anything difficult. She'll just tell me to act like a lady or something."

"You're wrong."

His words stung. Lacy stopped walking for a few seconds, then hurried to catch up. "Did she once ask me what I planned to major in, when I was home at Christmas?"

"You didn't give her a chance. You've been avoiding her ever since you started high school, as if there was something wrong with her. She excused it as teenaged angst, but it's time to grow up and start acting like a mature adult. One who's mature enough to decide her own future."

They strode down the lane in silence, while Lacy considered this. Was he right? When had she last had a real conversation with her mother? Had she ever told her about her dreams? It seemed like they always fought about her clothes and her tomboy behavior.

When Lacy didn't answer, her father added, "She deserves to know the adult you. Talk to her. Tell her how much you love math and physics."

They reached the end of the lane, and turned around. Lacy thought about his words the whole way home.

When they reached the porch, Lacy looked at her father, a question in her eyes.

"I won't tell her," he said.

She squared her shoulders. Perhaps she'd taken to eavesdropping because she didn't have the guts to confront her mother, but, if she was going to become a physicist, she'd have to be brave.

AFTER SHOWERING AND changing into a clean sundress and sandals, she went to the kitchen, where her mother was fixing dinner.

"Hi, Mama." Lacy lightly kissed her cheek, careful not to muss her mother's carefully-applied make-up. "Any mail for me today?"

Grumbling a bit, Maggie wiped her hands on her apron. "Yes. I put it in my purse. I'll get it."

When she returned, and handed Lacy the grade report, Lacy saw that her major was listed at the top. Even if it hadn't been, her As in calculus and physics would have been a dead giveaway.

Lacy looked up from the report. Her mother's eyes were hard, her mouth drawn.

"Dad told me," Lacy blurted out, before she could think about it. "You don't want me studying in a STEM field. You think I should do something more feminine. English Literature, perhaps?"

"Lacy—"

"No, Mama, listen. I like math. I like physics. And I'm good at them. You saw my SATs, and you've seen all of my grade cards. Remember? I'm the kid who wanted astronomy books and a telescope when I was ten."

"But why not nursing? Or—"

"I'm not demeaning nursing, or whatever. It's just that the laws of the universe are what draw me."

"Sit down, please. And listen to me." Her mother indicated the little kitchen table in the corner.

Lacy sat, her hands held tightly between her legs, certain she'd be told there was no way her mother would continue paying her tuition. "I'm listening."

Her mother took a seat opposite her. "I love you, despite what you may think. And I understand that women do sometimes succeed as engineers, lawyers, and scientists. I'm not saying they don't. It's not what they did when I was growing up, here in Georgia, of course—"

Lacy started to interrupt, but her mother shook her head. "Let me finish. And you know I still believe ladies should be mothers and wives first."

"Mama, that's so backwards. I'm not doing that." Lacy pushed her chair away from the table. This couldn't be happening. She had to get out of here.

"Stop running away." Her mother's sharp tone caused Lacy to sink back into the chair, but she looked down at the brightly-flowered table cloth instead of meeting her mother's gaze.

"Someday, I expect, you'll want to marry and have children."

"Maybe."

"Do you have any idea what that will be like, if you're off pursuing your grand physics career?"

Lacy shuffled her feet. Where was her mother going with this?

"It'll be hard. Don't think for a minute that your husband will cook and take care of the children while you go to work. It doesn't happen."

"So? We'll have a nanny——" Lacy picked at the table-cloth's edge, then put her hands under her legs.

"Don't count on it. And don't think you'll get the same promotions and the same salaries as the men. That won't happen, either."

She looked up at her mother's worried blue eyes and held her gaze. "I've seen the statistics. I've talked all of this over with my advisor. She's a physicist and she's really great. I know it's harder for women than for men, but I love physics. I want to be an astronomer."

Her mother pushed back her chair, stood, and took a step towards the counter, then returned and leaned towards Lacy, placing her palms on the table. "It's just … Oh, I worry for you. What if no man wants you?"

"Because I'm a nerd? Is that what you're really worried about? I can't change who I am. I'd be a nerd even if I majored in fashion design."

Her mother sighed. "Well, I don't know."

"Believe me. I would."

Just then her father walked in the door. "Is supper ready? I'm starving."

Her mother wiped her hands on her apron. "We're talking, Harold. About Lacy's future. Something we should have done a long time ago."

He nodded. "Want me to leave?"

"No." Lacy wanted him to help her out. "I was just telling Mama how much I want to be an astronomer."

"I don't understand it, Harold."

"That's because I was afraid to talk to you about it, Mama. You seemed so intent on teaching me manners, and going to all the right events, and so bothered when I mentioned my science classes, that I kept quiet."

Maggie bit her lip and picked up the potholders which had been lying next to the stove. She checked something in the oven. "The roast will be ready soon." Closing the door, she leaned against the counter, the potholders still in her hands. "How long have you known, Lacy? No, don't answer that. I suppose it doesn't matter."

Harold looked at his wife. "You should have seen this coming. She takes after my brother, always curious about the inner workings of things."

"I still think it's a mistake. She's too young to make a choice like this on her own."

I'm a college student, aren't I? I make my own decisions every day. But she kept those thoughts to herself. They would only aggravate things. To hide her scowl, she went to the pantry and took out a clean apron.

"She's almost nineteen. And this is where her heart is," her father growled. "We have to let her make her own mistakes."

Maggie sucked in her lips, her face grave, and took a deep breath. "I don't like it. It seems like just yesterday that I was putting her hair in pigtails. But maybe you're right."

Lacy clutched the apron to her chest. Had her mother really admitted she'd underestimated her and treated her like a young child? She grinned, and hugged her mother, the apron squeezed between them. "I'll make you proud. I promise." She let go and pulled the apron over her clothes, then twirled around the room.

Her mother laughed. "It doesn't help when you act like a little girl. I said 'maybe.' Remember, we're the ones paying your tuition."

But Lacy was sure she'd win this battle. She had to.

Maggie shook her head. "Set the table. We'll talk about

this some more."

Smiling to herself, Lacy opened a cupboard and pulled out a stack of plates for dinner. The matter of her college major wasn't settled, but at least she'd have a say. Tomorrow, she promised herself, she wouldn't hide behind the column: she would walk right out onto the porch and take a seat, and see what happened.

FLASHBACK

ROSEMARY STAYED IN the shower as long as she dared, sighed and turned it off. Delicious steam filled the room, even after she'd dried her hair, but she didn't have time to linger. They were expecting her at her father's retirement party in less than an hour. She needed to be on time because the table decorations and her father's present from the symphony were in her car.

She turned on the fan and cracked the door to clear the mirror so she could apply her makeup. While she waited, she went into the bedroom and pulled on the blue dress she'd bought for this special occasion. With her complex role of daughter, office manager, and member of the second violin section, she wanted to look her best, not just to show her father how much she loved and respected him, but also to show the world that the Redding Symphony was not failing. "No, Mr. Donor and Ms. Reporter," she practiced, "losing our concertmaster to the Northwestern String Quartet does not mean we are faltering. In fact, we will be auditioning for the post next week. After twenty years, my father is simply ready for something new."

She hoped no one would ask her anything more difficult than that, but they invariably did. She could parry the ones about who had applied to be concertmaster, since that was secret, but not the more personal ones. "What's it like to have such a famous father?" always made her cringe, because she heard *and be such a lousy violinist yourself* as the subtext. How exactly could she answer that? With the truth? If she said, "Nah, I don't have the patience to practice the same thing over and over again until it's perfect," or "I don't love classical music," at a gathering of symphony musicians and supporters, they'd descend on her like a nest of wasps, and she'd lose her job for sure. One had to act as if orchestral music, especially as played by their symphony, was the only music that mattered; in fact, one had to act as if it were the *only* thing that mattered.

Irritated by her worries, she inserted her long sapphire earrings, the ones she thought of as her armor against wealthy patrons and nosy orchestra members. Somehow, just donning them reminded her that she had plenty of practice answering these questions. She would be fine tonight, even when someone naively asked if she was applying to be concertmaster. As if she'd have a prayer of getting an audition.

She rolled a brand new pair of pantyhose onto her legs. Truthfully, she only played in the symphony because her father loved having her there, and she loved talking about their rehearsals and performances over late-night dinners with him. Soon, he'd be gone. What then? Did she want to continue sending out fund-raising letters, organizing rehearsal space and concert venues, and all of the other details she did for the symphony?

Well, she would have to face that question later. *Focus.*

She stepped into her heels and went into the bathroom. Her heart skipped a beat. An elderly, wrinkled woman gazed at her from the mirror. Rosemary blinked hard and looked at her hands. They were perfectly normal. Her arms were young and smooth, as were the legs which poked out below her dress.

What was going on? Was this an LSD flashback? She'd never had one, but she'd read they happened. She'd certainly dropped plenty of acid in her college years, and even tripped a couple of times since then. But those experiences were nothing like this. Instead of a kaleidoscope of color like she'd experienced on LSD, everything except the face in the mirror appeared the same as always.

Please, she begged herself. *We have to leave in fifteen minutes. Pull yourself together.*

Nothing changed. The old woman in the mirror still stared at her. Rosemary gulped. Maybe drinking some water would clear her mind. If she could find the kitchen.

Stumbling down the hallway, nothing else in her house seemed out of place. Her husband, already dressed, watched football in the family room. His mass of black hair poked over the top of their recliner. It looked completely normal.

Time was getting short. She went on to the kitchen, gulped a large glass of water, and returned to the bathroom. The old woman still stared at her. She had wrinkles covering most of her face, bright blue eyes, and long wet grey hair. Rosemary smiled, the old woman smiled too. Rosemary touched her ear, the woman touched hers.

No. No. This is not me.

She closed her eyes and ran her hands over her face. It had its usual fullness; no dips in the cheeks like the woman in the mirror. Opening her eyes, she saw that the hair falling over her shoulders was silky and brown. She took a deep breath. The illusion of the old woman, if that's what it was, was confined to the mirror, but that didn't mean she, Rosemary, wasn't going crazy.

Old or not, I have to get ready, and I'm not going without my makeup.

Gritting her teeth, she filled the makeup sponge with her foundation cream and faced the mirror. Her elderly reflection stared at her with the same frightened expression Rosemary suspected she sported. Seeing how scared the old lady looked, Rosemary calmed a little. This was simply some kind of illusion; one she didn't have time to explore. She applied her makeup, even though it proved difficult as the ancient woman leaned forward, copying her every movement, with one terrible exception: the brushes and pencils dipped into one wrinkle after another, the colors all wrong for an elderly, washed-out complexion. Rosemary just hoped her real face would look okay.

As she turned away from the mirror, she heard a voice. "Listen, Rosemary."

Shit, now I'm having auditory hallucinations. She wanted to run, but she felt frozen in place.

"It's time for a change," the voice said. "If you stay in

your current job, you'll turn into a bitter old lady, like this."

As if she were a doll standing on a motorized cake stand, Rosemary's whole body slowly rotated until she was staring into the mirror. The face looking back at her was much like the one she'd seen before, but its wrinkles ran downward from the corners of the mouth and nose, and deep furrows between the eyebrows showed her such unhappiness that Rosemary buried her face in her arms.

The voice spoke once more. "What about your dreams? Rosemary froze but the voice continued. "Where have you put them while you've been taking care of everyone else's? If you follow them, this is what you'll look like in fifty years."

Against her will, as if the woman's words held such strong power that she could operate her like a rag doll, Rosemary's head came up out of her arms. This time, Rosemary the woman in the mirror had smile wrinkles crinkled around its eyes. This was a woman Rosemary would enjoy spending an afternoon with.

"The choice is yours." The illusion faded.

Rosemary groaned and glanced at her watch. She blinked. The hands hadn't moved; she still had fifteen minutes, yet her second hand ticked at its normal reliable pace. The alarm clock by the bed said the same thing.

Huh? How did all that take place outside of time?

Rosemary didn't believe in magic, yet, maybe... She shook her head to clear it and double-checked her makeup, which looked fine. Going into the bedroom, she sat on the bed to collect her thoughts, now that she had an extra ten minutes.

It was true that she'd only dropped out of her rock band and moved back to Redding to help her parents. But what else could she have done? Her mother's cancer treatments had been difficult, and both her parents had needed her. She'd stepped into her mother's job with the symphony when the chemotherapy made her mother too weak to do the job, and she'd kept the position even after her mother felt well enough to work again, because her mother didn't want it anymore.

What were her dreams? Love, of course, which she'd found three years ago when she met Keith. Children some-day, but not quite yet.

Keith stuck his head in the doorway. "Rosemary? It's almost time to leave. What are you doing?"

She told him about the vision.

He sat on the bed and put his arm around her. "Let's go. We can talk about this on the way."

While they drove, Keith pointed out that her father had

resigned his position to follow his heart and his violin to something he'd always wanted. "You should, too. Since I met you, you've talked so much about your college years in Boston and singing lead in The Wondrous Ladies. Do you have any idea how your eyes light up with the memories? I've kept my mouth shut, because you seemed so determined to keep doing what you're doing, but why not try again?"

Her arms folded, her mouth tight, she fought against his words. Those were fantasies, unrealistic fantasies, ones which didn't pay the bills. Besides, who would she play with, and who would listen to her? Redding was a small, conservative city.

They arrived at the venue and she put the dark thoughts away in the rush to get ready for the reception. After checking on the caterers, she carefully placed each table decoration, with its miniature musical instruments, on the cloth-covered tables. By the time she'd finished with those and put the largest arrangement on the podium, the first guests had arrived. It wasn't until she sat next to Keith on the way home that she voiced her misgivings about finding musicians who would and could play her unusual compositions in this small city. "I did try, you know, when I first moved back."

He glanced over at her. "We don't have to stay here. I can

work anywhere."

"But we have friends. We own a house."

"We can sell it. We'll make new friends. I haven't said anything, because I knew you wanted to be near your folks, but I wouldn't mind living somewhere else."

Some tension released inside her. "Oh. Well, how about Austin? I've always wanted to check out the music scene there."

He smiled broadly, his eyes on the road. "Sure. We can take a trip. See if we like it."

"Or Nashville."

"Sure. Wow, I never thought I'd pry you away from here."

His words opened up a space inside her as inviting as a high mountain meadow in summer, yet she knew it wouldn't be as easy as he made it sound. "What about money?"

"What about it? We'll get by somehow. We have my income and we have each other. Come on, Rosemary, for once, let yourself do what you want."

Tomorrow the doubts would arise again, but for the moment she felt ready for anything. She pushed a CD into the stereo and sang along, her voice clear and strong.

THE FAVOR YOU DIDN'T MEAN TO DO

NOT IN HERE, I say, and lead you outside into the dusty, grassless yard of the rundown student house I share with three other college seniors, where I face you and cross my arms.

Your once-familiar sour sweat wafts towards me as you reach for my soul, a soul which no longer belongs to you, perhaps never did, and I step away: away from the two years of no word from you, away from the night when you broke our engagement so you could explore your options, that night when I vomited my despair into your parent's toilet with your mother worrying over me, unable to believe her son could hurt this girl she'd hoped would be her daughter-in-law.

My arms wrapped tightly around my body, both from

cold and self-protection, I wonder how to tell you of the favor you did me when you set me free. Sure, your rejection of our young love, of the promise you made when you placed that ring on my finger, hurt and burned, but I healed: I came to see that my world with you would have been too small.

Too small, because you, with your scorn for book-learning, and your decision to join the navy right out of high school, could never have made enough space for me, a college girl with aspirations for a career in science. And I, with my need to explore the knowledge of scholars, would never have been big enough for you, with your desire to sail the seas. All this and more would have caused our too-early-union to explode, leaving us both deeply scarred.

You showed up today, unannounced, somehow believing that our two years together outweigh our over two years apart, not seeing the naiveté of the belief that we could always love each other. Certainly, we had fun, but wasn't it an illusion that the great divide between us could be managed? An illusion I believed in until you stopped our merry-go-round that summer night and I got off, dizzy and sick. You have no idea how I cried myself to sleep for months and stumbled shell-shocked and lonely to classes, because you didn't stick around to find out, did you? Nor did you learn how, without you, and with the yeast of new friends and experiences, I eventually grew far away from that young girl you once wooed so desperately.

Even so, I feel a deep sadness when I tell you, a person to whom I gave my virginity back when I still believed in our love, that we cannot try again. I leave out all of the parts about our incompatibility, and only tell you the reason I believe you can understand—I have moved on and am in love with another.

Your jealousy and anger flood over me, your nasty words against the new lover you have never even met creating a wall I will never care to breach again in this lifetime, and I spit furious words in defense of my choices until you leave me alone in this dismal yard.

THE HOARDER

HER FATHER'S VOICE crackles across the line. "Can you come? It's nearly time." His voice breaks. "I know it's for the best, but——" He stops speaking again, and a little sob escapes him.

"Oh, Dad." Sarah imagines him, old and frail, alone in the house she grew up in, dealing with her mother's death. The line stays quiet for what seems like a long time.

"You still there?" she asks. International connections are so unreliable.

His hoarse whisper comes over the line, "It's hard to believe she's going."

"I know, Dad." Although she doesn't. She's been ready for her mother's death even before her mother went to the Alzheimer's unit seven months ago, and certainly since the call a month ago that her mother's kidneys were failing.

She scrawls a list of things she needs to do before she leaves: pay bills, arrange transportation to lessons and sports for the kids, get food, get ticket, call work. She can manage. "I'll be there as soon as I can, Dad. I love you."

He sobs and she stays on the line until he quiets and says, "She's hurting pretty bad. She won't eat."

Having spent two years working in a hospice center right after she became a nurse, Sarah knows that sometimes it's a relief when the loved one dies, but her father clearly doesn't feel that way.

As soon as she hangs up, she walks down the hall to Aiden's office, where he works from home most days. He swings his chair around to face her.

"That was Dad on the phone," she says. "Mom only has a few days."

He nods. "I'll hold down the fort. The kids'll be fine."

"I could be gone a couple of weeks. Dad's pretty upset. You know how much he loves her, despite everything. He'll need my help."

"He's your father. Of course you need to help. Stay as long as you need."

"Thanks, hon. I appreciate your support."

Leaving him to his work, she goes into the kitchen and calls the Melbourne hospital. The shift supervisor sounds angry at the short notice, but Sarah doesn't have any patience for these bureaucrats who make her life a nightmare, switching her schedule around so often she almost can't keep track. "You can drag me to work from Indiana, if you need me that badly," she sputters.

Then she calls a travel agent. This time of year, she learns, it is spring break in the States, and airplane seats are full of tourists searching for warm beaches.

Sarah wonders what part of 'my mother is dying' the agent didn't understand, but the agent comes back on the line after a few minutes. "The first available seat is two days from now."

"I'll take it. Let me know if there are any cancellations."

"Will do."

By the time she's returned from the store with enough food for her family for the next two weeks, the kids are home from school. She gathers them in the room with Aiden and tells them about their grandmother. "I want to get there before she dies."

"But we need you," Lillie, who is thirteen, but still not independent, protests. "What about my concert next week?"

"I'm sorry, honey. Your dad will have to go without me."

Fifteen-year-old Isaac shrugs his shoulders and pulls his hand free. Old people's problems don't bother him. "Don't be such a baby, Lil."

"But what if the plane crashes?"

"It won't," he says in the bored voice he's recently adopted. For once, Sarah is glad he's become so blasé. He'll pretend he doesn't miss her, and tease Lillie until she drops her clingy act.

THE TWENTY-TWO hour trip from Melbourne to Indianapolis seems longer than it was the last time, six years ago. She barely sleeps. Going through customs in Chicago is more of a pain than ever, but, finally, she's in her home city. She calls Aiden to let him know she's arrived, then stumbles, exhausted, to the luggage carrousel, where her father's brother Steve, who lives in Boston, meets her.

"Where's Dad? Did Mom——"

"Not yet, hon. Unfortunately, Gene fell yesterday afternoon and broke his fibula. He had surgery this morning; they put in a plate and screws."

There's a sinking sensation in her chest. Her poor father. How could he break his calf and have surgery while she was on the plane? At least it wasn't his hip; she knows all too well how dangerous a hip break can be for a man his age. "Where is he? I want to see him."

"In the hospital. We'll go straight there from here."

After grabbing her bag, she follows her uncle to his rental car, and they drive out of the parking lot. Once they're in the right lane, he explains that her father had been climbing on piles of newspaper and magazines, trying to find something, when he slipped. "Luckily, he had his cell phone with him and dialed 911."

"Wait. Why was——"

Her uncle stares straight ahead, his knuckles white on the steering wheel. "Looking for something, apparently."

"On top of a pile of newspapers? He's eighty-six years old, for God's sake."

"Yeah, well, tell that to him. Besides - well, you'll see."

"I'll see what?"

He checks his mirrors and doesn't answer, which alarms her more.

"I'll see what?" Something bad is happening, she senses it in her bones.

Uncle Steve is quiet. He grips the steering wheel hard and stares straight ahead, as if focused on the traffic. Clearly he doesn't want to tell her anything; he wants her to see for herself. She changes the subject. "Who called you?"

"He did, from the emergency room while he was waiting for the doctor."

She shakes her head. This is a mess. "I'm glad you came. How's he doing?"

"Groggy from the pain meds." Her uncle pulls onto the heavy traffic of I-70, heading towards the center of Indianapolis. He settles into a lane. "It's a bad break. They don't know if it will heal."

"Oh, my poor father. I imagine he wishes he were with Mom, instead of in a hospital bed."

"Of course he does. By the way, I know you were planning to stay at the house, but I don't think it's a good idea. I booked you a room at my hotel."

Again that sinking sensation, this time in her stomach. "What's wrong with the house?"

Her uncle clears his throat and changes lanes. "We'll go over there after we visit Gene."

Twenty minutes later, they park and walk into the hospital. "This way." Her uncle steers her into the elevator, then, when they reach the third floor, down one of the long halls. The familiar smell of antiseptic and illness greets her.

Her father's door is open. A television blares on the wall. He's on his back in one of the beds, a large cast on his left calf, which is propped high on pillows, his face grey and slack. An ache fills her chest. He's too thin, visible evidence of how difficult the past three years since her mother's dementia started have been on him.

"Look who's here," her uncle says.

Her father turns towards her and breaks into a smile. "My girl." He flicks off the television and pats the bed. "Sit by me."

She takes the spot he indicates and kisses his cheek. "Hi, Dad."

With effort, he raises himself on an elbow. His eyes swirl from the pain medications, and he winces when he shifts his leg. "How's my favorite girl? And my grandchildren?"

They talk about her family for a little while, before he points at his cast. "Stupid of me, but I want to bury your mother in the necklace I gave her for our wedding. I was hunting for it when I fell."

She doesn't ask why he was clambering over newspapers; she already suspects hoarding. There's been a lot of publicity about it lately. "I'll find it."

"Thanks, sweetheart. While you're at it, there's a framed

photo of the four of us, taken right before the accident. Can you look for that, too?"

"Of course." The accident. The one which changed everything.

SARAH REMEMBERS THAT day vividly. Not the morning or afternoon, of course. She had no idea what she'd had for breakfast, or what they'd covered in her classes.

But she can never forget the feel of the first warm day of spring floating through the windows and her nineteen-year old brother dropping the keys to his new car on the kitchen table before going into his room to change from his school clothes into worn out jeans and a T-shirt with the sleeves cut off.

She'd followed him. "Where you going?"

"For a drive."

"Take me. Please." She'd longed to ride in his Mustang, maybe even drive it. She had her learner's permit, after all.

Peter had rubbed her head hard with his knuckles, something she hated. "Not today. Let me work out the bugs first. It's an old beater. It don't run good. But soon. I promise."

The rest of the afternoon was a blank. More than likely, she'd done homework until the phone rang. "This is the

Indianapolis Police Department."

"Mom," she'd shouted. "Mom, I think you'd better take this."

Peter had driven too fast around a corner and lost control of the car. He'd hit a tree. An ambulance was at the scene.

The rest of the day had gone by in a rush. They'd raced to the hospital and discovered that Peter was in a coma and bleeding profusely. As soon as her mother signed the papers, people in white wheeled him into surgery. Sarah would never forget that last glance of him on a gurney, gray and still. Her father arrived soon afterward and took her home, then left to keep her mother company. Peter hadn't lasted the night.

WHEN SHE AND Uncle Steve arrive, the old house looks good from the front, a blue-grey ranch with white trim and a recently mowed lawn, but, as soon as they open the door, she smells mildew. Stacks of magazines line the walls of the living room, nearly touching the ceiling in places. Bottles and bits of metal, along with stacks of fabric bolts, fill her old bedroom, nearly three feet deep in some places. Her parents' bedroom is clean and organized, but junk crowds the rest of the house, with narrow pathways from one room to the next. She wonders why the whole place hasn't gone up in flames.

She pushes the door open to her mother's project room, and a stack of newspapers falls on her head. She doesn't dare open Peter's door; no one has opened it in many years. It'll be the same as the day he died, only dustier.

Her uncle, right behind her, says, "This is your mother's doing. It used to be worse, before she went to the Alzheimer's unit."

Remorse fills her. "I can't understand why Dad didn't tell me. I had no idea. I mean, I knew she was never quite right after Peter died, but she was never this bad."

Her mother had stored everything her brother owned and wouldn't let them take even his clothes to a thrift store. His bedroom became a shrine. Everyone understood that, but what became obsessive was the way she treated whatever Sarah touched. It all went into plastic bags and boxes. Every homework assignment, every book, every shirt was wrapped up and stashed away; she photographed Sarah constantly, as if she could hang onto her every moment.

Sarah had gone to Australia two weeks after she graduated from high school, partly to escape this. She'd understood her mother's fear, but she just couldn't stand the way she'd snatch a piece of paper off the floor and pack it away. "Mom, it's just a grocery list," she'd say, to no avail.

Her uncle folded his arms. "When did you last visit?"

"Five, no six years ago." And they'd stayed in a hotel, figuring two rowdy kids would be too much for her parents. Had she peeked into the bedrooms, the couple of times they'd come over for dinner? Probably not. The hoarding could have started by then. If she were honest with herself, it could have been going on since she'd moved away. She'd only been home a few times since she moved to Melbourne, and, always, she'd spent as little time in the house and around her mother as possible.

He sighs. "Gene loves your mother very much. He would never say anything bad about her." His face brightens. "I convinced him to let us throw out the junk, now that Gladys won't be coming home."

"He thought she might improve?" Perhaps her father was as delusional as her mother.

"Yeah, I know." Her uncle shakes his head.

"Let's order a dumpster." She goes to the drawer in the kitchen where her parents have always kept the phone book, and flips to the number. "Then I want to see Mom before I get some rest."

HER MOTHER IS a soft, still bag of bones who doesn't stir

when they come into her room and say hello. Sarah pulls up a chair and picks up her mother's limp hand. She squeezes, but there's no answering movement. Nothing at all.

Sarah's uncle clears his throat and indicates with his head that he'll leave them alone. Sarah nods, and he vanishes. She studies her mother's nearly-lifeless face and marvels at the way the robust lady who'd baked cookies and played with her grandchildren only a few years ago has turned into this shell. A few tears creep into Sarah's eyes. She tells herself it isn't because she misses her mom, it's because she's facing her own mortality.

"Mom, it's Sarah. If you can hear me, move a finger or blink."

Nothing. Even if her mother could react, she would not understand that her daughter had come. Sarah babbles anyway. "Aiden and the kids send their love. I'm going to find that photo of us with Peter, right before he died. What dress do you want to be buried in?"

After a few minutes, she rises. "I'll be back tomorrow."

In the hallway, she asks for an update on her mother's condition from the nurse. She is still hanging in there, but they don't know for how long. Sarah gives them her cell number, and they promise to phone if anything changes.

Then they drive to the hotel, where, after she checks into her room, she falls into a long, deep sleep.

THE NEXT MORNING, she and Uncle Steve visit her father, who has been moved to a recovery center, and is too tired and drugged to talk much. Leaving him to rest, they head to the house. The dumpster has arrived. All day, they chuck newspapers, magazines, and bottles, while Sarah keeps an eye out for photographs and jewelry. By the time they stop for dinner, they've cleared the hallway and the living room.

"That's enough for today," her uncle says, over burgers at the local diner. "This old body can't keep up the pace. If you want to continue, you can drop me off at the hotel and use the car."

Sarah's cell rings. She looks at the number and her whole body tightens. It's local, but not one she recognizes. She answers and the woman on the other end informs her that her mother has passed away.

The phone rings again. "Hi, Dad. I heard."

"Did you find the necklace?"

"Not yet, but I will. Don't worry."

"I've gotta get out of this damned place. Gotta get ahold of the mortuary and the funeral home." He sounds surprisingly organized and calm. Perhaps he's in shock, or he's reconciled himself to her death better than she'd expected. She won't know until she talks with him again.

"How are you?" She asks.

"So tired."

Definitely shock, she decides, perhaps combined with the drugs and post surgery. "I'll be by in the morning. Rest up, Dad." She has to find that necklace, hopefully tonight.

BACK AT THE HOUSE after dropping off her uncle, she opens the door to her mother's project room. If her father hadn't found the necklace in the bedroom, it must be in here. Slowly, she digs a tunnel towards the closet, hauling one garbage can full of bottles after another outside, until she reaches a wall of newspapers which touch the ceiling. Bringing a ladder into the room, she lifts a foot-tall stack to the ground and looks at it. The top paper is dated ten years ago.

She thinks back. The kids had been little six years ago, when they'd brought them to see where their mother had grown up. For the most part, their grandparents had come to the hotel to watch the kids play in the pool, or to take the family sightseeing and out to dinner. When she and her family had come to this house, they'd played games in the living room, or made cookies in the kitchen. Had her mother made some excuse about this room being off limits to children?

Sarah grimaces. She should have paid more attention, instead of focusing on her children and doing her best to avoid her mother.

She works her way down the first stack, then moves the ladder and starts on a second. It is older than the first, and there are even older newspapers shoved in behind it, brown with age. When did this hoarding start?

The doorbell rings and she goes to answer it.

"Hi, I'm Charlotte." An older lady stands in the doorway. "I live across the street. I saw the rental car and the light and wondered if everything is okay."

Sarah introduces herself and tells her about her mother's death and her father's fall.

"So sad about your mother."

"Thanks."

Charlotte pushes her way past Sarah into the living room. "I was afraid something terrible had happened to Gene. I tried to talk to the ambulance drivers, but they wouldn't tell me anything. I've called his home number several times and left messages, but I don't have his cell. I'm glad to know he just broke his calf."

Who is this rude neighbor? Sarah wants her gone. "I'm really busy."

Charlotte doesn't seem to hear the implication in her words. "I've gotten to be quite good friends with Gene, even though I'm the one who called the police last year. I felt bad, but I just couldn't stand your mother's screaming one second longer."

Her mother's screaming? Sarah gapes, torn between wanting to hear the truth and wishing this person would shut up and leave. "Mizz——"

"Oh do call me Charlotte. I won't stay long, but you need to know that your mother used to walk down the street in her nightgown, and tell everyone who tried to stop her that your father was an imposter who planned to rape and murder her. You have no idea what a toll that took on Gene. He wouldn't tell you, no matter how many times I insisted. He said you'd been through enough, that you had your own life now, and Gladys was his responsibility."

Sarah falls onto the couch and drops her head in her hands, trying to imagine her parents struggling, her father taking care of her mother as she lost all recognition of who he was. Charlotte's words run on and on like a leaking faucet, giving her a headache, until she lifts her head. "Please leave."

Charlotte ignores her. "I suppose you think I'm awful for what I did, but it was the best thing for him. He's slowly gained weight since they put her in that nursing home."

Gained weight? Her father is thin and drawn, all knobs and protrusions covered by a thin veneer of skin. If that is fatter, how skinny had he been? Why hadn't she realized how bad things were? Why hadn't her father told her? But she knows. She would have flown over and taken his Gladys away from him, to live in some cold institution, long before he was ready to let go.

Charlotte puts a hand on her shoulder. "You should stay with me. This house isn't healthy."

Fat chance of that. This woman has no boundaries. "I'm fine. I'm at a hotel with my uncle." She stands. "And I need to get back to work. I want this house cleared out before Dad is released." No way is she going to tell Charlotte about the necklace.

Charlotte looks at her, and her face is soft and concerned. "I'm glad you're here. I've told Gene a thousand times his house isn't safe. I'd offer to help, but the doctor says I can't lift anything heavy. My heart, you know."

Sarah squares her shoulders. "That's okay. I can do it."

Charlotte shakes her finger, as if scolding her. "Just like your father. Always got to do it alone. Well, I'll let you work." She heads to the door, then turns and looks Sarah in the eyes. "Make sure you let me know about the memorial service. I'll inform the neighbors; they all love Gene. And if you need anything, just ask. I'm right across the street." Her voice changes and raises into a question. "Would you like me to rally a few neighbors to help clear the junk?"

Sarah looks at her, a bit surprised by the offer. Perhaps this lady is more than a busy body. "Thanks. We could use help. My uncle's too old for this. Tomorrow. Tonight I have to find something."

After Charlotte leaves, Sarah sinks into the couch to rest for a few minutes and wakes to the insistent chirping of birds. Early morning light filters into the house through the windows. A sharp pain in her neck tells her she'd slept in an odd position. She stands, groggy, and works it out. It's after seven. She stumbles into the kitchen and starts a pot of coffee, relieved that her father buys beans from a local coffee roaster. While she waits for it to brew, she phones her uncle using the telephone on the wall.

He answers immediately. "I see you're at the house

already."

"I slept on the couch. Never found the stuff Dad wants. I'll come take a shower and change, then we can get breakfast. I want to check on Dad, too. I need to help him organize the burial and memorial service."

"I can do that, unless you want to have a say."

"Whatever Dad decides is fine with me." She should care, but she doesn't.

Two and a half hours later, she stands in her mother's project room and sighs. Newspapers still block the closet door. She is almost certain the necklace is there; she remembers her mother holding it over a shoebox, cutting the string to let the beads fall one by one into the box, then tying the lid on with string wound around and around, while she muttered angrily about the idiocy of allowing a nineteen-year-old boy to buy a run-down sports car. She'd shoved the box hard onto the top shelf and spat on it. "My marriage is a farce." Then she'd turned and seen Sarah standing in the doorway. "What are you staring at? Get out."

Her mother had stayed angry for years. She refused to cry at Peter's funeral, and, when she caught Sarah lying on his bed, wracked with sobs, had nastily told her to buck up and get on with her life. Over the years, the anger had seemed to fade; she'd taken obvious delight in her grandchildren.

Unable to make sense of it all, and unwilling to cope with the conflicting emotions these memories evoke, Sarah tells herself not to think and simply focus on the task ahead. She dismantles the next stack of newspapers and magazines, taking it armload by armload out to the living room, then tackles another one, until the living room looks almost as bad as it did yesterday when she arrived.

Switching gears, she heads to the curb with a load, and discovers that the dumpster is already almost full. She will need another one soon.

"Hello! Sarah!"

Charlotte comes out of her house, wheeling a handcart. "I couldn't find anyone to help this morning, but I did borrow this."

"You're a godsend. But I can't do much more until I get another dumpster."

"My grandson works for the garbage company. We'll have another one here in a jiff." Charlotte pulls a cell phone out of her pocket and punches at it.

Hurray for nosy neighbors. Sarah takes the handcart and heads inside. For now, she will continue piling the trash in the living room.

By lunchtime, she has a space cleared around the closet. She slides it open and stuff rains down, sending up a cloud of dust and making her cough. When the air clears, she sees that paper and boxes fill every inch of the little space. Great. It will take her hours to clear this out and check every possible hiding place.

Nothing for it, I'm gonna hand the necklace to my father today.

She examines the papers falling onto the floor around her and recognizes sewing patterns her mother used to make clothes for the grandchildren when they were little, a pattern for one of the dolls she'd sent for Christmas, and one for its dress. The thin papers send Sarah back in time, remembering how excited her mother sounded when the kids talked to her long-distance, remembering how cute they'd been. But she doesn't dare linger. She dumps a stack of the thin papers on the floor to get to a box. Inside, she finds photos of her with Aiden, Lillie, and Isaac, carefully stacked and labeled. A filing box holds her letters, organized by year in manila folders, and this, finally, makes her stop digging and go to the kitchen for more coffee.

Anger bubbles as she stands leaning against the counter, waiting for the microwave to heat the already-stale brew. *How dare Mom cling to these traces of me and my family, when in person she was so awful to me? I had to be her emotionless soldier,* *because she couldn't deal with Peter's death.* Any time she'd tried to talk about her love life, her difficulties with employment, or, heaven help her, Peter or her father, her mother cut her off, with a dismissive wave of her hand and a sharp, prim voice. "You must deal with your own problems and emotions. Now, what are we having for dinner?"

The microwave dings, and Sarah retrieves her mug. She sips, trying to reconcile that mother with the one who played Candyland on the rug during her parents' Melbourne visits and so obsessively saved her letters. And when had her mother stacked all of that trash in front of the closet? She must have had it elsewhere and moved it there when she realized her mind was going. But why? Some misguided attempt to hide her sentimental side? It would have taken a huge effort.

Her head swirling with the questions, her body aching from the heavy lifting, she returns to the closet.

Shortly after noon, the doorbell rings. The closet is nearly empty. She's found more letters and photos, and boxes and boxes of her clothing, from her baby shoes to her prom dress, but no necklace and nothing relating to Peter.

Her uncle comes to the door of the room. "Tried to phone, but you didn't answer."

"I didn't hear it."

"I brought sandwiches. Hope that's okay."

"Sure. Dad's not with you?"

"No. He's tired. They've decided to keep him another day."

"Oh, that's good. I don't want him in the way while I toss the garbage. He can look through everything that's worthwhile later."

It's warm enough that they take the food into the backyard and fill each other in on their mornings. "Your mother's funeral is set for the day after tomorrow. She'll be buried in that blue dress hanging in your father's closet, and her black pumps."

"I thought the necklace would be where she shoved it years ago, but it isn't there. If I do find it, it will have to be restrung."

"Your father will be pretty upset if you can't find it. He talked about it constantly while I drove him around this morning: how pretty your mother looked in it, how it set off the blue in her eyes, how she wore it every day until Peter died."

She finishes her sandwich and takes a slug of cold coffee. "I should get back to work."

"I promised to go by a florist and order flowers."

"Mom loved yellows and oranges. Mums, especially."

"That's what Gene said. I'll see what I can do."

AFTER THE CLOSET is empty, Sarah runs her hands along the top shelf. Nothing. This is crazy; the necklace could be any-where. This room is still crammed with stuff, her old bed-room is filled to the gills, as is the attic and one side of the garage. Who knows what's in Peter's room.

Think. This was Mom's sanctuary. It has to be here. What would I do if I lost Lillie or Isaac and I no longer trusted anyone? It dawns on her that her mother had a mental breakdown after Peter died, one she hid behind sharp words. Given the way she'd cut up that necklace, and caught Sarah watching, she'd have looked for somewhere safer, as if she were a raven or a mur-derer. Could it be in the yard, under a bush? Biting her lip, she decides against that. Her father was an avid gardener. Her mother would have been afraid he'd notice any freshly dug earth and ask about it.

It's in this room. Under a floorboard. Or....

Retrieving a flashlight from the kitchen, where it was still stored in the same place it had always been, she shines it into the top of the closet. The usual drywall ceiling had been removed and replaced with a plywood board, fastened to the bare two-by-fours above with at least a hundred nails and two metal bars screwed over it—the work of a crazy person, determined to prevent anyone from breaking into her secret stash. *Eureka.*

Her father has a toolbox in the garage. She retrieves it and pulls over the ladder. Standing as high as she dares, Sarah unscrews the bars. Getting the board off is a different matter, for many of the nails are buried deep in the soft wood. She tries banging it with a hammer, but it won't crack. Then she tries to grab an edge with the hammer's claw, but that doesn't work either.

She hears a motor, then a grinding and looks out the front window to see what is happening. A truck is raising the old dumpster. She goes outside to watch and talk to the men clustered around it.

"Thanks for getting here so fast."

One of them stares blankly at her, then seems to realize what she's talking about. "Oh, I'm not with the garbage company. I live two houses down. I heard you might need help?"

"Yes. I do. Do you own any tools?"

He's a large bald man, about thirty, with a thick black

beard. His brown eyes crinkle into a smile. "I'm Jared. Just got off work. I'm a contractor. I have plenty of tools. What do you need?"

She explains.

"I'll be right back." He sticks his hands in his pockets and saunters down the street.

Shortly after the garbage men set down the new dumpster and drive away, she goes inside for a glass of water. In the bathroom, she realizes that dust clings to her face and hair, turning her normally honey brown hair and eyebrows to white, and highlighting the little wrinkles which grow from the sides of her mouth. Is this how she'll look when she's old? She finds a clean towel in the hall closet and washes her face, even though it will quickly be covered in dust again.

Footsteps sound in the hallway, then in her mother's room. It takes Jared about fifteen minutes to remove the board. He shines a light into the space above the closet.

"There's some stuff up here. Do you want me to hand it to you?"

Some stuff turns out to be eight large packing boxes set on plywood boards in a ring around the hole. She takes them from him as he lifts each one down, then sends him to the living room to haul trash to the dumpster.

The first box she opens is full of her parent's wedding photos, cut to bits. The next contains family pictures. They are whole, at least the ones with her and Peter; the rest are crossed out with black ink or shredded. She pieces a few together, trying to ignore the sadness which wells up like a geyser. This mutilation must have taken her mother many hours.

Framed photos fill another box, this time untouched, and the photo her father wants is on top. She lifts it out and sets the box aside with a sigh. She paces the cleared part of the room, then goes outside to stand in the yard, unsure if she can face the remaining boxes. She wishes she had a drink, something very strong. A bird flies past, carrying a piece of string for its nest. Its babies will grow up and fly away for good. No elderly parents to fuss with. For a second, she is almost envious.

Sarah returns to the room and gingerly opens another box. To her relief, it is full of Peter's baby clothes and toys, instead of more ruined memories. Pink journals fill the next box. She recalls her mother writing in them, lounging on the couch or sitting at her desk. Sarah opens the top one and wishes she hadn't.

Counselor says I must write about what happened. But I can't. The date was September 14, 1961, two months before her parents' marriage. The rest of the page is blank, but Sarah flips to one which contains a bombshell. *His disgusting big hairy body, with fishy-smelling wet skin pimply and albino white under the hair, his face covered with a black mask. Is that what she wants me to write about? Watching him pull out that knife and stab Peter? My beautiful, beautiful Peter?*

Who was Peter? Sarah keeps reading, even though these are her mother's private thoughts, not to be shared with anyone. Most of the pages are full of rants, sadness, relief that Gene wants to marry her, his best friend's girl, so she won't shame her family by bearing Peter's child out of wedlock. She sits back on her heels, in shock. She's read about such things, but never thought they pertained to her family. No one had ever said a word, and her parents never acted like they didn't love each other, at least not before her brother's death. Her *half* brother's death.

Sarah tells herself she should stop reading and find the necklace, but she can't. She skips over the bit about raising a child, until she finds a journal dated right after her own birth. The first statement, *this baby will bind us, and heal the past,* causes her to stop breathing and set the journal back in the box. Her mother had wanted to love her father. Maybe she even had succeeded, but, when Peter, her love child, died, it must have brought back the trauma.

She can't read any more. Inside the final packing box, she finds the shoe box she's been looking for, still wound tightly with string. Cutting off the string with a knife from the kitchen, she finally sees the loose beads from the necklace. There are also pages torn from one of her mother's journals. *Can't love him anymore, though I try my best. How could he let Peter buy that car? And poor Sarah; she's lost her mother and gained a hungry ogre afraid to let her out of its sight. It's broken. It's all broken, and I am lost.*

Her poor mother. She'd blamed herself for … what? Being unable to comfort her daughter? For being mean to her father? For clinging so tightly? No wonder she had been afraid of losing the memories of her children. Sarah shuts her eyes and cries for her mother, for herself, and for her father. She realizes that she'd never let herself feel the depth of the tragedy, not just the loss of Peter, but what it had done to herself and her parents, turning them into strangers. And she'd compounded the issue, by closing down and running away to Australia. That must have hurt both of her parents.

Once she calms a little, she pours the beads into her hand and feels their coldness and then their warmth as they take on the heat from her skin. She makes herself examine them, the glass beads which hold such power for her father. They symbolize all of the love he'd pledged to her mother, even though she was pregnant with someone else's child. Who had this woman been that he could love her so much?

Another memory surfaces, of her mother dressed for a night out with her father, sitting on her bed, reading a story to her, and acting it out. Sarah had adored her mother then, her face so happy and full of love. And they'd laughed and laughed. It had been a terrible shock to be screamed at after Peter's death, because her mother had never been like that before.

Sarah thinks about her own children. If Isaac died the same way Peter died, how would she react?

I forgive you, Mom. I wish you were still here, so I could say I'm sorry to you.

She pulls herself together. She has very little time to get a jeweler to restring this necklace. But she feels softer and less defensive than she's felt in years, so first she calls Aiden and her children to tell them how much she loves them.

THE NUMBER OF people at the funeral surprises her. Her aunt Henrietta and two of her cousins attend, along with her uncle, but the rest are friends of her father. When she files past the open casket, she sees why her father wanted the blue dress and the necklace: her mother is beautiful in them.

Once she returns to the spot beside him, she watches her frail, elderly father as he says goodbye to the love of his life. Tears pour freely down his face. This is a man who is not afraid to give his whole heart to others and to show his emotions. Peter's death tore him to pieces; she remembers him wailing and beating his chest. But his love for her and her mother never wavered. How had he managed to do that, even when her mother blamed him for the accident and withdrew from him into hatred and madness?

She sees the way people gather around him as they leave the church, and considers how lucky she's been; for many more years than she'd realized, he'd spared her the truth about her mother's mental state. He'd saved her thousands and thousands of dollars by bringing her mother to Australia for visits instead of the other way around. A soft warm wash of love fills her, and she promises herself she will stay until his house and garage are clear of trash and his leg is healed. Her children and husband don't need her as badly as he does.

PHOTO SHOOT

THE DANCER BENDS over her foot, tying the pink ribbons around her ankle. In her filmy white tutu she looks like a painting by Degas.

Belinda snaps one photograph after another, fuming to herself. Why has she been given this trite assignment, when Amy, with half her experience, is over at Grenador Hall, recording a truly avant-garde event? Hasn't the world seen enough photos of skinny ballerinas in fairy outfits?

"Turn slightly towards me," Belinda orders, "and up a little. That's it."

Click, click, she uses up half a roll of film, then orders the girl, for she is just a kid, even if she is the star of this show, to stand and hold some poses with one leg high in the air. She has to admit that she herself could never do the splits, even on the ground, let alone like this, but photographing it is all so trivial and done.

She reorganizes the light, changes cameras, and shoots fast. She zooms in close because at least this ballet star—what is her name—oh, yes, Zelda—has an interesting, long, narrow face, and an arrogant air. This makes the assignment slightly less annoying. Most ballet stars have, in Belinda's experience, overly pretty faces to go with their overly pretty bodies and poses.

"You are bored. We do some radical moves in this piece," Zelda speaks for the first time, her accent thick. "They aren't so pretty."

Belinda tries to recall where Zelda is from. Russia perhaps? She should have paid more attention when her boss gave her the background for this afternoon's session. It is an important event; she remembers that much. A premier.

"Show me a little," she says.

"I'll dance a bit. Stop me when you see something you like, okay?"

"Fine." Belinda walks over to lean against the wall. She's photographed lots of dancers, but rarely gets to see them in action.

Zelda goes into the center of the room and stands very

still, in fourth position. Belinda yawns. Nothing radical in that. The first few turns and leaps look like any other ballet, she thinks. But then Zelda surprises her by jerking into a position with her legs wide apart, her knees bent, still up on her toes. She swings forward onto one leg, almost looking broken, turns quickly, and slumps onto the ground.

This is no normal ballet, Belinda realizes. Her interest is piqued. She leans forward, watching carefully, as the dancer lifts herself off the ground and swings her legs wildly, leaving the skirt of her tutu on the floor, to reveal fushia-colored gym shorts.

The camera, so much a part of her that she hasn't even realized she's lifted it to her eye, is clicking. This is good stuff. She can't ask Zelda to stop; she could never capture all this energy and madness in a pose. Zelda is still on point, falling and catching herself. Her hair loosens out of her bun, covering her shoulders with thick black curls; she rips her bodice off to reveal a black tank top, a tattoo painted on her upper back. The running shorts come off, leaving her in tight black lycra shorts. She's a pop star now, still in pink point shoes, still throwing in a ballet move or two.

Sweat pouring off of her, Belinda doesn't let herself think, she has to become one with this dazzling creature if she wants to capture her on film. She runs, chasing Zelda and the light.

It's over. Zelda, like some creature of the night, prances off the stage, except it wasn't the stage, only the dance studio. She returns, panting, to where Belinda holds her cramped stomach, trying to catch her breath.

"You okay?" Zelda asks.

Belinda moans. She promises herself that she will start working out. Tomorrow.

When she can breathe easily again, Zelda hands her a cup of water. She gulps it quickly. "Where did you learn to do that? I thought you were a ballerina?"

Zelda shakes her head. "That was Contemporary. You liked it?"

Belinda nods. "It was fabulous. Amy is going to be so jealous. Don't worry." She clasps her camera to her chest. "I got what I need."

"Good. Too bad Charles and the rest aren't here. It's much better with the other dancers."

"They all dance like that?"

"At times. It's wonderful. But you should see the entire piece performed on the stage. I'll comp you tickets."

"Oh, thank you. But I don't just want to see it. I want to

learn how to do it."

"You almost did." Zelda laughs. The sound is surprisingly deep, but sweet.

Belinda studies her. Zelda's older than she'd realized, perhaps mid-thirties. Her narrow face shows expressions easily, quickly ranging from joy to seriousness. A series of portraits flashes through Belinda's mind. They would make a wonderful addition to her portfolio.

"Could I take some close-ups of you?" she asks. "Your face is so interesting."

"No, that is not allowed."

"Why not?"

"We only use the authorized portrait."

"I could hire you for a photo shoot. I wouldn't show anyone else."

Zelda holds up her hand. "No. I have a contract; I cannot do something professional unless the ballet authorizes it, and they would never say yes."

Belinda takes her camera off and unscrews the lens. Time to go. "What's the dance about?"

"What do you think?"

"Women coming into their own. No longer being pretty objects for men to admire."

"Women's power." Zelda nods. "Although, believe me, traditional ballet is much more difficult to perform. It takes more strength and skill to look like dust fluff and do everything perfect than to look strong and do unusual moves. In this piece, we can make small mistakes and no one knows."

"I would never guess that."

"Have what you need for your magazine?"

"Yes, yes, I think so."

"Good. Well, I look forward to the article. Two tickets enough? Opening night?"

Belinda nods. "Thanks."

Clearly dismissing her, Zelda goes to the bar and bends over it in a way which looks unnatural. She's ridiculously flexible.

Belinda packs up her lights and cameras, then realizes she has another question.

"Where could I learn to dance like that? I mean, not that, but just a little something like it?"

"Tomorrow morning at eight. Beginning modern for adults."

"Are you teaching?"

"No, but the instructor is excellent. It's good you are a true beginner. No bad habits to fix."

Belinda nods, before heading to the car. She'll look fat in her workout clothes, but she cannot betray the ache that started in her chest when Zelda jerked into that first, non-ballet-like position.

PROMOTING KINDNESS

NATIONAL PUBLIC RADIO. August 12, 2067.

TRANSCRIPT OF TODAY'S SHOW:

KINOA JEN: We begin today's show with the sad news that one of the great women of our times, former governor of Oregon, Geraldine Foster, passed away last night. Born July 26, 1969, she had just turned 98. In honor of Ms. Foster, whose actions inspired millions, we bring you a special report from Kim Tiada, her official biographer. Kim?

KIM TIADA: Thank you Kinoa. This is a very sad day for all of us who knew and loved Geraldine Foster, and a great loss for the country and the world. I will miss her. My condolences go out to her only living relative, her granddaughter, Olivia Howard.

Because Ms. Foster was such a powerful and articulate speaker, I present her in her own voice. What follows are excerpts from our first two interviews, which took place at her home, where she lived until yesterday with her granddaughter, Olivia Howard.

When I arrived at their small house in Bend, Oregon, Olivia and her grandmother were in the front yard, picking straw-berries. Ms. Foster was a tall, thin woman with piercing blue eyes. Her curly white hair had once been the same bright red as Olivia's. They showed me around their garden, then led me into the living room. I waited on a threadbare armchair while Ms. Foster changed into a sweatsuit and began stretch-ing on a handmade wool carpet.

[TAPE BEGINS]

KIM TIADA: Thank you for agreeing to speak with me, Ms. Foster. I've never interviewed anyone who insisted upon stretching while we talked, especially not an eighty-eight-year-old.

GERALDINE FOSTER: You don't mind, do you? My old body gets stiff if I don't do this at least once a day.

KIM TIADA: Please, go ahead.

GERALDINE FOSTER: I shall. What's your first question?

KIM TIADA: You've led a fascinating life.

GERALDINE FOSTER: Don't push me into the grave. It isn't over yet. Although I'm no longer living on the world stage, I still enjoy things.

KIM TIADA: I see that. Did you make that rug?

GERALDINE FOSTER: Me? Ha. It was a gift. It's goat

hair, from a local farmer. You should get down here with me. Be good for you.

KIM TIADA: Umm, I'm wearing a skirt.

GERALDINE FOSTER: I'm sure Olivia could find something for you to wear.

KIM TIADA: No thanks. Don't mean to be rude, but I doubt I could interview you and exercise at the same time.

GERALDINE FOSTER: Suit yourself. So, what do you want to know? Shall I start with my birth?

KIM TIADA: Not that far back. People know you as a political figure, but before that you were a nurse, weren't you?

GERALDINE FOSTER: A nurse practitioner, an NP. Worked at a health clinic for low-income individuals for over thirty years. Raised two kids by myself.

KIM TIADA: What about your husband? Didn't he help?

GERALDINE FOSTER: We divorced when our youngest - that's Olivia's mother, Shawna - was two.

KIM TIADA: Does that mean that he wasn't around at all?

GERALDINE FOSTER: I don't know you at all, young lady. Let's stick to politics today. We'll get to my personal life later.

KIM TIADA: All right. At what point did you become politically active?

GERALDINE FOSTER: Ah, yes. It's going to sound odd, but it was the local food movement that got me started.

KIM TIADA: What was that?

GERALDINE FOSTER: You really are young. I bet you weren't even born until after things collapsed.

KIM TIADA: True. So explain, please.

GERALDINE FOSTER: It's going to sound rather silly to you, since everything is grown locally nowadays, but agricultural companies used to ship food from one country to another.

KIM TIADA: Why'd they do that?

GERALDINE FOSTER: To make money, of course. They'd grow it in some developing nation, usually a warm one, where land was cheap and regulations were lax. Poor farmers with no other options would work the fields for pennies.

KIM TIADA: And they used fossil fuel to ship it?

GERALDINE FOSTER: Right. Yet another reason that global warming got so bad. And there were other problems; they used loads of toxic chemicals to control weeds and pests.

KIM TIADA: How did they get away with that?

GERALDINE FOSTER: The way people always do. Bribes. Corruption. Force. Anyway, the local food movement was a reaction to the chemicals and the shipping, plus it tapped into a desire to be self-sufficient. We wanted to encourage local farmers and home gardening.

KIM TIADA: Didn't people already grow what they needed

here?

GERALDINE FOSTER: Are you kidding? We'd always had very short summers, with cold nights. That was changing by the time the local food movement started. But when I was young it could freeze hard any day of the year. We used to laugh at those who had home vegetable gardens; they were fools. Even our Farmers Market pretty much only carried stuff from The Valley, over a hundred miles away.

KIM TIADA: Strange. Now most food goes the other way.

GERALDINE FOSTER: Right. They get too much rain. They always got a lot, but not like now.

KIM TIADA: So tell me about the local food movement.

GERALDINE FOSTER: It was a worldwide phenomenon. The idea was to stop all that importing. Instead, we'd support local farmers by buying their produce. It was a little tough to do that in Central Oregon when we started.

We didn't grow much here, like I said—as I recall there was one guy who sold things like greens and turnips—but the movement took root. People figured out how to extend the season with greenhouses.

There was even a couple who grew the impossible: beautiful tomatoes. They started selling them around 2010, maybe a little earlier, and oh, they were a rare treat. I still remember biting into one for the first time and being surprised by the burst of flavor.

KIM TIADA: Why did you get involved?

GERALDINE FOSTER: My children were little then. I

worried about what they ate, and what was in it. It seemed crazy that we bought apples from New Zealand. When a friend of mine started an organization to connect buyers with local farmers, she asked me to help.

KIM TIADA: And that was your first involvement in politics?

GERALDINE FOSTER: In organizing something big, yes.

KIM TIADA: Then what?

GERALDINE FOSTER: Gradually, rising temperatures extended our growing season. Not a lot, but a week or two on either end makes a big difference. Warmer nights made a big difference, too.

KIM TIADA: And?

GERALDINE FOSTER: Don't push so fast for the bottom line, Kim. I'm an old woman.

KIM TIADA: You sure don't act like one. You're more limber than me.

GERALDINE FOSTER: I really should make you do yoga. Everyone should do this every day.
[LAUGHING]

KIM TIADA: Continue.

GERALDINE FOSTER: Our location, near the ocean but just east of tall mountains, meant we were spared some of the worst effects of the warming—the catastrophic storms and flooding. We also reaped the benefits; our season was much longer than before and we no longer had hard frosts in the middle of the summer. We had water, too. That meant we could grow more variety more reliably. It was great not to rely on the rest of the world so much for basic foodstuffs.

KIM TIADA: Which meant more and more people moved here.

GERALDINE FOSTER: They sure did. They came to get away from the heat, the flooding, the crazy weather extremes, and the diseases. Before 2022 or so, it was mainly the very rich and well-off retirees. There were also a lot of outdoor enthusiasts who came to play in the mountains and desert. The area grew fast, but not so fast that we couldn't absorb everyone. However, when things deteriorated else-where, that changed.

KIM TIADA: When was that?

GERALDINE FOSTER: The first wave came after that big storm destroyed cities all up and down the Pacific Coast. That was in 2024. Did you study that in History class?

KIM TIADA: Sure, but I don't remember the details.

GERALDINE FOSTER: No matter. Probably forty—no, more like fifty-thousand—showed up here within a month of the storm, with only what they could carry in their vehicles.

KIM TIADA: Cars?

GERALDINE FOSTER: Cars, trucks, motorhomes, moving vans. And they just kept coming.

KIM TIADA: So that's when you decided to do something?

GERALDINE FOSTER: I probably should have started

then, but no. I still had Shawna at home to think about, and,
I don't know, I guess I thought they'd all go back to where
they came from once the flooding ended. The country was
still intact then. We had FEMA, which was a government
agency which handled emergencies. And I was right; a lot of
the people did go home once the worst was over, and the
federal government helped their cities rebuild.

KIM TIADA: But that's when the first clashes erupted.

GERALDINE FOSTER: Yes. Since this area is kind of
isolated, it was hard to get enough supplies. The Red Cross
and FEMA did their best; they set up camps for the evacuees
and tried to feed them, but soon the newcomers were spread-
ing out, looking for housing, and settling in. A group of
locals freaked out and started policing the camps with guns.
If you couldn't prove you were from around here, you
couldn't leave the camp, unless you were willing to be escort-
ed out of Central Oregon.

KIM TIADA: And people snuck out?

GERALDINE FOSTER: Of course. They found places to
live, landlords and real estate agents willing to look the other
way if they could pay the price. At first, the locals who were
determined to keep them out just shouted at them, but then
there was a shootout at an apartment building, and things
escalated.

It was a scary time. I wouldn't let Shawna—she was still in
high school—leave my side. I even bought guns and we
learned to shoot.

KIM TIADA: And your son?

GERALDINE FOSTER: [SIGH] He was already in Boston, in his second or third year at MIT. We worried about him, but there was nothing we could do, other than email or phone to check on him.

KIM TIADA: Were you personally involved in any of this? I heard there was an attack on your clinic.

GERALDINE FOSTER: That was later, in 2029. Things had settled back to normal, somewhat, but, every once in a while a gang would try to commandeer resources. We were attacked by some men headed through the area on their way to Canada.

KIM TIADA: You were working that day?

GERALDINE FOSTER: Yes, I was.

KIM TIADA: Can you describe happened?

GERALDINE FOSTER: By then, there had been enough trouble that the clinic's front door was kept locked. When patients arrived, they used a phone on the outside of the building to call the receptionist who checked their identification before letting them inside. We had an armed guard in the lobby at all times, too. So these thugs showed up, and, when the receptionist wouldn't let them in, they started shooting at the windows. We moved patients into the interior rooms as fast as we could. A bullet flew right over my head, and bounced off the wall. One hit the doctor next to me. I screamed and ducked, and hustled a couple of children to safety. Luckily, the guard had already phoned for help and it arrived quickly.

KIM TIADA: Much of the country didn't have phones by then.

GERALDINE FOSTER: Well, we still did.

KIM TIADA: How long did that last?

GERALDINE FOSTER: You mean telephones?

KIM TIADA: Yes, and all of the rest of early twenty-first century technology.

GERALDINE FOSTER: Gosh, I don't know. My cell phone died in 2032. So twenty plus years? Most of the cell towers had been knocked down by then anyway. I could hardly ever make a call. Landlines were probably kaput by then, too.

KIM TIADA: What about computers?

GERALDINE FOSTER: They all died, too.

KIM TIADA: Nothing? Nada? What did you do?

GERALDINE FOSTER: Honestly, we just learned to live without. We were doing without a lot by then. I'm not sure we're better off now that we have them again.

KIM TIADA: I'm hoping those holorecorders will come on the market in time for our next interview.

GERALDINE FOSTER: I'm not. Who wants to watch an old lady talk?

KIM TIADA: A lot of people. They all want to know about you. For instance, what happened to your daughter, Shawna, and your son, Leo?

GERALDINE FOSTER: After college, Leo moved to New York City. When the riots started, we lost touch with him.

KIM TIADA: And you've never heard what happened to him?

GERALDINE FOSTER: No. Not yet, at least. We've sure tried, but no one seems to know anything. If he were alive, I am certain he'd contact us, now that it's possible again. [SIGH]

KIM TIADA: I'm really sorry. Perhaps I can find out for you.

GERALDINE FOSTER: That would be lovely.

KIM TIADA: I read that your daughter was murdered.

GERALDINE FOSTER: More of an assisted suicide. She got breast cancer in 2042. It might have been treatable in the old days, but we just didn't have the means anymore.

KIM TIADA: I am sorry to hear that.

GERALDINE FOSTER: We didn't even have morphine to manage the pain. She begged us over and over to shoot her. Her husband finally gave in. He shot her and then vanished.

KIM TIADA: That's awful. How old was Olivia?

GERALDINE FOSTER: Nine. The whole affair was awful. It was horrible for her. She watched her mother suffer and lost both parents at once. Then she had to live with everyone accusing her dad of murder.

KIM TIADA: I'm sorry. I didn't mean to—

GERALDINE FOSTER: I know you didn't, but it's what the

world believes. It's your job to let them know the truth. I've tried. [BIG SIGH]

KIM TIADA: How were you able to go out and do so much after losing both children?

GERALDINE FOSTER: I did it to honor them. To make a world where other mothers wouldn't have to lose their children. I ... I'm sorry. [SNIFFLING] I ... I need to stop.

KIM TIADA: Of course.

[TAPE ENDS]

KIM TIADA: Well, Kinoa, as you can hear, the former governor was too overcome to continue.

KINOA JEN: Totally understandable. Who can talk about their children's deaths without becoming upset?

KIM TIADA: Not many.

KINOA JEN: I heard that you managed to find her son Leo.

KIM TIADA: Yes. It took me two years, but I finally located him. Alive.

KINOA JEN: And Leo had been very ill.

KIM TIADA: Right, Kinoa. He'd contracted a number of illnesses, including cholera, malaria, and Lyme, which had left him with brain damage. When I found him, he was living in Pennsylvania with people who didn't know who he was, because he'd forgotten his own name.

KINOA JEN: And you tracked him down him and brought him to live with his mother.

KIM TIADA: Yes. He was still quite ill. Ms. Foster and Olivia nursed him, but he never fully recovered. He died six months later.

KINOA JEN: So sad.

KIM TIADA: Yes. Still, those few months were happy ones for Ms. Foster.

KINOA JEN: What a good deed, Kim.

KIM TIADA: Thank you. It was worth it.

KINOA JEN: I understand that you have another interview for us.

KIM TIADA: I do. This is from the following week. We continued where we left off. I've cut out about ten minutes of the beginning this time.

KINOA JEN: Okay, let's hear it.

[TAPE STARTS]

KIM TIADA: Getting back to 2029, that's when you proposed your plan?

GERALDINE FOSTER: Oh, no, dear, certainly not. Remember, as an NP in a public health clinic, I worked long hours. I figured I was doing enough.

KIM TIADA: So, when?

GERALDINE FOSTER: Slow down, woman. Don't push me.

KIM TIADA: Sorry.

GERALDINE FOSTER: You want to hear the story, don't you? I'm old. Who knows how many more interviews I'll do for you?

KIM TIADA: [LAUGHING] Continue. What happened next?

GERALDINE FOSTER: As the ramifications of climate warming continued, more people moved here. I saw the situation up close. Many of the newcomers came into our clinic. They had diseases we'd rarely seen before: malaria, dengue fever, worms, Lyme Disease, all kinds of stuff. I looked around at the mess, at hunger-crazed people going into fields and stealing crops in the middle of the night, crying children dying of starvation and diarrhea, and my heart felt heavy.

One night, a group of migrants broke into our yard. Shawna and I peeked through the curtains and saw children stuffing food from our garden into their mouths like wild animals. They ate muddy carrots and bug-infested cabbages. Adults stood at the gate, making one batch of kids leave so another could graze. Once the vegetables were gone, the children pulled worms out of the ground and ate those. We were appalled, but it got worse: a group of local vigilantes appeared and went after the poor children with baseball bats and whips. The vigilantes even shot at the adult migrants.

Shawna and I ran out of the house, screaming at the vigilantes to stop, but they ignored us. They chased the migrants down the street. In the morning, there was a note on our door warning us to stop helping the riffraff.

KIM TIADA: But you didn't.

GERALDINE FOSTER: I still wasn't ready to do more than my job at the clinic. But, within a week of the raid on our garden, that was in 2031, a newly-formed governing body for Deschutes and Crook Counties—those are the local counties, which amazingly still exist—passed a resolution requiring people to prove residence for longer than five years. If you couldn't do that, you would be deported. They posted volunteer guards on the roads in and out of the area to keep out the unwashed hordes. Anyone who slipped through the barriers was shot. It was nuts, as if the Mexican border had moved just down the road from us.

That cruel decision made me angry, maybe for the first time. The migrants were desperate. Many of them had lost family and friends to the heat waves rocking the country. Others'd lost their homes from flooding or fires. There were small children and pets among them. What had happened to our sense of compassion?

In any case, the migration had only just begun. I'd followed news about climate science for years. Things weren't going to get better for a long time.

KIM TIADA: You were right about that.

GERALDINE FOSTER: Unfortunately. Anyway, I got the idea that we should allow a few in at a time. They would have to agree to build houses for each other, sort of a Habitat for Humanity approach – well, of course you don't remember that organization. It's been gone for twenty years at least.

KIM TIADA: You're right. Never heard of it.

GERALDINE FOSTER: Scratch that reference. I talked to co-workers and friends, and they liked the idea. We came up with a plan to present to the authorities. The migrants would build groups of small houses or apartments around a central square. The square would have a community garden and either solar panels or windmills. There were lots of carpenters and electricians and other builder types among the migrants. We knew, because they always talked about their past lives when they came into the clinic. They'd have to go elsewhere for their supplies, of course, but that really wasn't a problem. There were loads of abandoned buildings all over the country that they could strip.

KIM TIADA: I read that some of the locals pitched in to help them.

GERALDINE FOSTER: Of course we did.

Anyway, at first it was just an idea. But we told it to more people, and they got excited. They told others. Soon everyone seemed to have heard some version or another, so we organized a meeting. I stood up in front of the city council and made our modest proposal to let in forty hand-picked families. They voted no, without much discussion.

KIM TIADA: That must have upset you.

GERALDINE FOSTER: I don't remember. I kind of think we expected it. We were just planting a seed. I do remember that we didn't let it stop us. We went to the county commissioners. They took us a little more seriously, but then voted no, too.

Still, a large number of locals eventually supported the idea of the pods. Sure, there were those who argued that we were in for trouble, that our region couldn't handle more people. They argued that times were hard. We couldn't possibly feed them. What would we do if they turned on us and attacked?

KIM TIADA: All good points. We studied those years in school. There were large gangs roving the country, with lots of ammunition, killing, raping—

GERALDINE FOSTER: I know. But the people who wanted to live here weren't like that. And most Central Oregonians have kind hearts. They hated sending sick kids away. By now, the Red Cross and FEMA had disappeared, so it was up to us to help, if we could.

KIM TIADA: So, after you succeeded, you were elected to the county commission and then the state senate before becoming governor of Oregon at the ripe old age of seventy-five.

GERALDINE FOSTER: You make it sound so easy. [BITTER LAUGHTER]. It wasn't, believe me. Do you want to hear my whole story, or not?

KIM TIADA: Oh, of course.

GERALDINE FOSTER: Central Oregon was attacked many times before those roving gangs realized they couldn't get away with much here. We had a pretty good local militia. On top of that, pretty much every adult in Central Oregon had at least one gun. The county had also stockpiled grenades and other weapons.

There was one bad attack, though—honestly, I thought we were goners.

KIM TIADA: What happened?

GERALDINE FOSTER: Not long after we made our presentation to the county, a militia arrived with tanks and all kinds of advanced munitions. They recruited some of the migrants who were camped just outside the area and equipped them. They swarmed in, and took over a number of ranches and the entire town of Prineville. Then they used drones to bomb Bend. Blew up the hospital and city hall and marched towards the city in a great wave. Civilians took refuge west of the Deschutes River. The local militia hunkered down along the river banks and eastern sections of the city and lobbed bombs at the invaders.

As the bombs landed on them, their migrant recruits scattered, leaving only around a hundred gang members. Our militia wiped them out over the course of a week. Those of us who lived east of the river went home and cleaned up the mess left by the invaders. We were a lot wiser and more alert to the dangers after that.

KIM TIADA: That attack must have made people less willing to try your idea.

GERALDINE FOSTER: Actually, it did the opposite. It made them realize that the migrants were our best defense against marauders. If we trained and fed them, they'd help defend the area, instead of attacking us. The county com-missioners approached me and asked me to organize con-struction of a trial pod.

KIM TIADA: And you did?

GERALDINE FOSTER: Yes. I gave up my job to do it. By then, I was ready to retire anyway.

KIM TIADA: How'd it go?

GERALDINE FOSTER: I wanted people I'd met through the clinic before the area was sealed off, but locating them——well that wasn't easy. They'd scattered: some had gone south, some north. A few were even hiding out in the mountains. We did our best to send word through the grapevine.

KIM TIADA: And you found them.

GERALDINE FOSTER: Enough. We tried to keep the project under wraps, because we didn't want to be deluged by hungry families. But eventually we had our first meeting, and the project got underway. We had loads of eager volun-teers from Central Oregon for the first and second pods, and the twenty families we selected pitched in. A couple of guys even made several trips to California in a solar-powered truck and scavenged building supplies. It was amazing, really.

KIM TIADA: I bet you were pleased.

GERALDINE FOSTER: It was hard work. Harder than I'd imagined. Not physically, because I didn't do the building and the digging. But the organizing——I sure made lots of mistakes. There were two families we had to kick off the project because they started fighting with each other, and another one that tried to take control and change things. That meant we had to select three new families half-way through.

It took six months to get that first pod up and running. Once we were finished, the newcomers were such wonderful people that the county let us do two more.

That time, we grouped the forty new families into committees, each with its own responsibility: from building to coordination to security, food, and sanitation. The families from the first pod were put in charge and required to help build the new ones. We were amazed at how well that worked, I can tell you. It sure kept everyone out of trouble. No one had time to sit around idle, at least not until the houses were finished, and the gardens planted.

KIM TIADA: What about the dire warnings that these new people would just be more mouths to feed?

GERALDINE FOSTER: They were wrong. The first pod provided food for the second two. And on and on, after we were allowed to keep building pods.

KIM TIADA: I read it was self-sustaining.

GERALDINE FOSTER: Sort of. Once a pod was built, its members had to at least help build the next two. Responsibility, we found, turns people into good citizens pretty quickly. Plus, they knew they would be kicked out of the region if they messed up.

KIM TIADA: No violence?

GERALDINE FOSTER: We had less than we'd expected, perhaps because the county took everyone's guns and ammunition when they entered. If they behaved, they got their weapons back after a few months.

KIM TIADA: Weren't they afraid of being attacked while they weren't armed?

GERALDINE FOSTER: Of course they were. But, after that gang in 2033, we never had a large one come in here. A couple of small ones snuck in through the mountains, but they were easily repelled.

KIM TIADA: Amazing. How did you know this would work?

GERALDINE FOSTER: I didn't. And I don't want to make this seem like it was easy. Fights often broke out in these little pods. The apartments were tiny, so people were on top of each other all of the time. They built grudges. People can be awful, you know, and poverty makes them worse. While we did our best to inspire a sense that we had to work together to survive, emotions often ran high. One time a former university professor was assigned to shovel next to a high school dropout. By mid-afternoon, they started whacking each other with their shovels and had to be pulled apart. Several times, neighbors started affairs. Those often turned ugly.

KIM TIADA: How did you deal with disputes?

GERALDINE FOSTER: I organized a meeting with everyone involved and try to mediate them. Sometimes, I decided to swap families from different pods. Since no one owned much, it wasn't too difficult to move them. But I hated having to be the one in the middle. I was relieved when a professional mediator took over from me.

KIM TIADA: How did the area manage with all of these new people as the climate grew warmer? I heard there were some terrible drought years here.

GERALDINE FOSTER: True. The rivers dried up sometimes, but we sit over a reservoir. We were able to pump enough to keep going and water our crops. Lots of kale and potatoes, as I recall. To this day I can't stand either one [CHUCKLE]

There were deer in the mountains—the local government legalized hunting them without a permit. More and more people had chickens, goats, turkeys and other livestock.

KIM TIADA: And medicine?

GERALDINE FOSTER: [SIGH] We never had enough. A few local labs re-tooled to produce antibiotics, needles, steroids—real basic stuff. People died of things we could have cured easily before. I used to cry myself to sleep, unable to stop thinking about the children. Then, when Shawna got cancer . . . if it weren't for Olivia, I might have put a bullet in my own head.

KIM TIADA: I'm glad you didn't.

GERALDINE FOSTER: [CLEARS THROAT] Well . . .

KIM TIADA: At least we have good care again, and plenty of pharmaceuticals.

GERALDINE FOSTER: I keep forgetting that you weren't born when this happened. Phew. It was bad. Sometimes the county commission would make people bring medicines and other supplies before we'd let them into the area. They'd find them faster than we could believe. People badly wanted what we had created.

KIM TIADA: We're running out of time today, so I want to jump ahead and get a general outline of your political career. I heard that you were asked to be a county commissioner.

GERALDINE FOSTER: Not exactly. [CHUCKLE] A few friends asked me to run for the position. I had strong opposition from those who thought we should have shot the migrants, and from some of the immigrants who were used to being in charge and wanted to run the show. I've always thought politics a dirty business, but I started to realize what would happen if either of those camps took charge, so I finally gave in to the pleading.

KIM TIADA: You won, of course.

GERALDINE FOSTER: Barely. I did that for one term, starting, I believe, in 2038—well, I'll have to double-check the dates for you. Then I sat on the Joint County Safety Board for two terms. After that, I decided I could do more good in Salem, so I ran for the state senate, then for governor.

KIM TIADA: By then, cities all over the country had adopted your ideas?

GERALDINE FOSTER: Apparently. I don't know how they

all found out about it, with communication lines as bad as they were. Even Canadians tried pods. Anyone who could tried to move somewhere livable. Chaos erupted as waves of people migrated into the good places. We could have had that here; we almost did. But our——I'm not going to take credit for everything——our plan worked. Word spread and other areas tried it. Then more and more until we finally had a fragile peace over most of the continent.

KIM TIADA: You were like a war hero.

GERALDINE FOSTER: Hardly.

KIM TIADA: Or Ghandi.

GERALDINE FOSTER: Good grief. Don't put me on a pedestal. It's too lonely up there.

KIM TIADA: Yeah, but here you were, already what many would consider old, and you did so much. How did you manage?

GERALDINE FOSTER: I suppose because it was fascinating to discover new talents when I was in my seventies. However, when I finished up my second term as Governor at the ripe old age of eighty-one, I was ready to hand the helm over to someone else.

[NEW VOICE]OLIVIA HOWARD: Grandma, you're tired. Ms. Tiada, it's time to stop. She needs her lunch and then her nap.

GERALDINE FOSTER: Fine. I used to lead the whole state, but now my granddaughter tells me what to do. Can you believe it? Will you be staying for lunch, Kim?

KIM TIADA: No, no. I'm headed back to the office. Thank you so much for your time.

KIONA JEN: Thank you, Kim, for those wonderful recordings, and for your insights into this amazing woman.

KIM TIADA: My pleasure, Kiona.

THAT WAS GERALDINE Foster, in 2057, who died last night at the age of 98, speaking with her biographer, Kim Tiada. The steady hand of former Governor Foster, who was a close advisor to our current President up until the last few months, will be sorely missed.

Look for Tiada's biography of Ms. Foster early next year.

You can find film and holographic footage of Governor Foster at NPR.GFoster.holo.

BELLA'S REBELLION

I'M SO EXCITED! I checked a mystery novel out of the library this afternoon, *Death by Strangulation,* the third one in the Dr. Franks series. I hope it's as wonderful as the first two. Hubbie is out of town, so there is no one to complain if I read all night.

I should eat dinner, but forget it! I pour myself a glass of rosé and crawl into bed, stuffing all of the pillows behind my back. Sylvester curls beside me, and I rub his fluffy cat body before savoring a sip of wine. Then it's story time.

Stony Meadows, the amazing author of these mysteries, wastes no time in preliminaries. On the very first page, the town drunk finds a woman's body while rooting for food in a dumpster. He drops the half-eaten chicken in his hand and runs to his buddy's house, his teeth chattering in fear.

I'm hooked. That poor woman. What if the drunk doesn't tell anyone, and she ends up buried under a ton of trash? I'm so engaged, I barely notice that Sylvester has crawled onto my lap.

I read on. The drunk's buddies convince him to report the death, even though he's afraid he'll be fingered for a murder he didn't commit. Or did he? I, of course, wonder, but that would be too easy, wouldn't it? I trust Ms. Meadows to lead us on a long chase before we piece the puzzle together, just like in her previous novels. In any case, I hope the poor guy won't turn out to be the killer, as he seems sweet.

After a little back and forth with the police, they follow the town drunk to the dumpster, where they retrieve the body. The medical examiner determines death by strangulation, with a good old-fashioned clue left behind——a fresh tattoo on the right hip. When the woman is identified as a twenty-one-year old drug addict, the cops figure a pimp or drug-dealer killed her. Dr. Franks, on the other hand, reads the autopsy report and thinks something doesn't add up, which confirms what I've deduced.

I gulp more wine and work out a kink in my neck. Sylvester yawns and licks my hand, his sandpaper tongue reminding me of his presence. He's getting heavy, but my discomfort isn't enough to break my concentration for more than a second. I leave him where he is and continue reading.

Dr. Frank examines the body at the morgue and finds the tattoo, the same one a patient of his sported a few weeks previously. Ah, I think, right along with him, this is suspicious, and, sure enough, he takes a photo and tracks down a well-known tattoo artist, Bella, to ask her if she knows anything about it.

I'm so deep into the story that I don't even realize I have finished my glass of wine when the next sentence peels off the page. All I manage to read is "Bella strode," before the words solidify into a woman lying on the bed next to me.

I rub my eyes, wondering if the wine has a higher alcohol content that I'd realized, but, if so, the effect is incredibly strong because I feel her weight on the mattress. Expensive perfume wafts towards me. I stare, so shocked to see this thin woman with bright orange and purple hair materialize that I can't speak or move. A black and red tattoo curls up from her shoulder-blade, protruding out the top of a red tank top. For a second, I wonder if she will kill me, but then she rolls off the bed and walks out the door.

Suddenly, I come to my senses. "Wait," I shout. "Where are you going?"

Bella turns and announces in a silky low voice, "I'm getting out of this plot."

I sit up straight. "What do you mean, you're leaving? You can't. This is a library book. I have to return it in good shape. Get back in there." I point at the now empty spot on the page where she is supposed to perform her bit.

"No way." She turns and takes a step. I jump off the bed, disturbing Sylvester, who doesn't seem to notice Bella, and go after her. She stumbles in her spiked heels, and I grab her arm.

"Why are you doing this?" I ask. "You're ruining my evening. I need to know how the story turns out."

She pulls at her arm, but I don't let go.

"I can tell you how it ends," she snaps. "I've lived through this piece of shit thousands of times, every single time someone reads it, and I always lose. I'm pegged as the murderer, when I'm innocent!"

She stops trying to escape my grasp and glares at me. "Dr. Franks is a fraud. He misses half the clues."

"How do you know?"

"You think that a book is just what is on the page. Well it isn't! We have a whole life that goes on behind the scenes. The stupid author ignores most of it. Last time someone read the book, I figured out who killed that young kid and how they did it."

"Oh, really!" I say, sarcastically.

"Of course. Let me go! I'm going to find a typewriter and fix this stupid plot so that I'm the detective, and I catch the murderer."

I release her, realizing that her version might be even more interesting than the original story.

"There's a computer in there." I point to the door. "Make yourself at home. Would you like some wine?"

"No way! I only drink martinis." She shakes her head haughtily and her many piercings sway back and forth. I stare at a tattoo of a cobra on her arm.

"We don't have any hard liquor."

"I knew it. My God, look at you in your flannel night-gown buttoned all the way, and your perm, so prissy. What are you doing home alone on a Friday night? You should be out, rocking the town. But, no, you're here, probably adding more lace to the house."

"I was reading. And I love lace." *How dare she criticize my style?*

"I wish I had my kit. A rose would be perfect right here." She touches the back of my shoulder.

I shiver, a little scared and a little excited by this wild woman.

"Look at you, your eyes are shining," she says. "I bet you'd rather have a cobra like mine than a flower."

She's right, although I'd choose a dragon instead—one with fire coming out of its mouth—but I don't feel like confiding that to this bizarre stranger. "Tea then?" I ask.

"Fine. I've never used a computer; you'll have to show me."

I make a pot of tea, then join her at the computer. She's already figured out how to turn it on, though by now I've begun to wonder why a magical creature like Bella needs a machine. I sit with her for a while, until she seems comfortable with my word processor.

"Thanks. Go rest," she says. "I'll be awhile."

Immediately, my mind fills with mist. The wine I drank earlier must be spiked with magic mushrooms because I barely make it to bed before I am asleep.

WHEN I WAKE at six, she is gone. I am certain for a minute that I dreamed the entire encounter, but the novel sits on the desk next to the computer. It has a new subtitle, *Dr. Franks Unmasked*. Inside the front cover, a piece of paper contains a drawing of the tattoo on Bella's arm, her signature, and the words "Thank you."

Wide awake, I settle into an armchair to read. Later today, I resolve, I will see about getting that tattoo.

ACKNOWLEDGEMENTS

I COULD NOT have written this book without the critiques and encouragement of my friends in the Sky Writers Facebook group, my co-authors from the Mosaic project, and my friends from shortfictionbreak.com. Special thanks go to Mirel Abeles, my editor for *Heritage* and *The Hoarder*, and the copy editor for the entire book. Special thanks also go to Jen Henderson, who has helped with so many aspects of this book, and to Jeff Elkins, founder of shortfictionbreak.com, who has believed in me from the moment we met during the Story Cartel course.

I am certain I am missing many people who have helped and encouraged me during the creation of this book, so many thanks to them, as well.

Thanks also to Albert Arguello, my partner, for putting up with many evenings of late dinners, and my absent-mindedness and terrible house-keeping.

Cover art is by Margie Deeb. Elaine Roughton edited *Robotics*.

ABOUT THE AUTHOR

ANN STANLEY'S SHORT stories and flash fiction pieces regularly appear in the online literary journal shortfictionbreak.com. Her stories have also been featured in several anthologies. She lives in the high desert of Bend, Oregon, where she hikes, skis, bicycles, gardens, and entertains her two corgis. who fervently believe she should stop writing and spend all waking hours doing their bidding. Despite their wishes, she is hard at work on her first novel.

In addition to being a writer, Ann in an accomplished musician. She has performed in a variety of bands and taught flute. She has a Ph.D. in applied mathematics, and spent many years researching the spread of HIV. For the past fifteen years, she has also worked as a massage therapist.

Learn more about Ann Stanley and download the free short story *You Gotta Have Friends* at:

annstanleywrites.com

You can find Ann Stanley online at:

www.annstanleywrites.com

Her blog:

www.annstanleywriting.wordpress.com

Her Facebook author page:

www.facebook.com/annstanleyauthor/

If you enjoyed this book, would you consider leaving a review online? Reviews are the way authors get found. Other readers use them to help decide what to read. It makes all the difference to independent publishers who rely on reviews to get found. Thank you!

A lot of time and effort has gone into the writing and editing of these stories. Still, mistakes happen. If you find an error, please contact Ann, so she can correct it.

For more stories by Ann Stanley, and a free copy
of *You Gotta Have Friends*, go to:

www.annstanleywrites.com